'What do y[...]
honeymoon v[...]
have a roman[...] a
rattlesnake.'

'Yes, well,' shrugged Jake. 'You'd probably be more at home with one. I'd agree...' He stopped suddenly. 'Why do you think we're supposed to be on our honeymoon here?'

'Some sort of sick joke, I expect,' replied Sara witheringly.

'Perhaps it's escaped your attention but we're here on a job.'

'Pretending to be on honeymoon with you!' she observed searingly. 'If you'd told me about this in London you could have had my resignation then and there.'

Jake, his grip tightening on her arm, swung her to face him. 'Why do you think I didn't tell you?' he demanded. 'You're not going to resign until I've finished with you!'

Sally Carr trained as a journalist and has worked on several national newspapers. She was brought up in the West Indies and her travels have taken her nearly all over the world, including Tibet, Russia and North America. She lives with her husband, two dogs, three goldfish and six hens in an old hunting lodge in Northamptonshire, and has become an expert painter and decorator. She enjoys walking, gardening and playing the clarinet.

Recent titles by the same author:

REBEL BRIDE

HONEYMOON ASSIGNMENT

BY
SALLY CARR

MILLS & BOON

*MILLS & BOON and the Rose Device
are trademarks of the publisher.
Harlequin Mills & Boon Limited,
Eton House, 18-24 Paradise Road, Richmond, Surrey TW9 1SR*

© Sally Carr 1996

ISBN 0 263 79820 8

*Set in Times Roman 10 on 11½ pt.
02-9611-55510 C1*

Made and printed in Great Britain

CHAPTER ONE

JAKE was coming towards her and Sara's heart gave a double thud. His eyes held hers as he walked across the office and she knew by the look in them that he was going to stop and talk to her. Knew, too, that she was not going to like whatever it was he was going to say.

She swallowed hard and tore her gaze away from his. So much had happened between them that she wished they could have met again anywhere but here in a newspaper office, where there was no such thing as privacy.

On the other hand, she reflected grimly, being alone with Jake these days was about as advisable as taking up lion-taming.

Sara rested the palms of her hands on the desktop and was appalled at how damp they felt. Still, after all that had happened, Jake was more likely to want to shake her by the neck than the hand.

Memories crowded into her brain and she tried desperately to shut them out. She had to keep calm. Had to.

He was getting nearer now, his long stride eating up the yards of carpet that covered the open-plan newsroom. Desperately she reached over to the fashion editor's desk, jammed next to hers in the features department, and grabbed a bottle of nail varnish.

With shaking fingers she unscrewed it and began to apply the glossy colour, trying hard to look as though she was completely absorbed in her task, but in reality not even conscious of the unsteady brush strokes she was drawing over her nails.

'Sara?' He was standing at her desk now, leaning on it and looking down at her. The timbre of his voice made her heartbeat more unsteady, her fingers more clumsy with the varnish. She knew exactly the expression on his face without even having to raise her eyes to his.

Once she had hoped he had loved her, and now she knew for certain that he hated her. She only wished that she could feel the same way about him. Could exorcise completely the surging pulse rate and the almost over-sensitive awareness that she had of his presence.

Silence seemed to draw out between them for several hundred years. She felt if she looked up she would find the entire office staring at them, aware of the almost tangible tension between them. But when she finally lifted her eyes to his face, she realized from the big clock above them that only thirty seconds had elapsed. And nobody but Jake was looking at her.

'Hello,' she said unsteadily, unable to hold his gaze. 'Can—' she licked dry lips '—can I help you?' She had meant to sound cool, dismissive, sarcastic. But the words came out high and cracked and she knew she sounded like a junior receptionist on her first day, instead of a supposedly sophisticated showbiz journalist.

Jake gazed down at her meditatively, but she knew better than to trust the expression on his face. Hadn't she been taken in by it so easily all those years ago?

And she was right. 'You mean like you helped my brother?' he said silkily. The menace in his tone all too apparent.

'Our brother, you mean,' corrected Sara huskily, feeling her throat closing at the memory of Jamie's death. She swallowed. She must not, must not break down in front of Jake.

'My father may have adopted you when you were five,' he grated, 'but you needn't think you're any part of my family. Not after what you did.' His eyes bored into her. 'And if I'd had my way,' he added dismissively, 'you would have been sacked long ago.'

Sara lifted her chin and stared at Jake as steadily as she could. 'Just as well you're only a photographer here, then,' she retorted, 'rather than taking over your father's position as chairman of the board.'

He gave her a look she didn't quite understand and then, almost as if they were friends instead of the bitterest of enemies, sat down on her desk and picked up the bottle of nail varnish.

'Leave it alone,' snarled Sara, her nerves twanging almost to breaking point.

'Purple,' mused Jake softly. 'To go with your prose style, I presume.'

'It's none of your business,' she screeched, grabbing for the tiny bottle. She had expected some resistance, almost as if she were a child once more and he was teasing her.

But now the long fingers gave way to hers almost as if they couldn't bear the feel of her skin, and the bottle slid from her hand and splashed down the front of her skirt.

She stood up in horror, gazing speechlessly at the sticky purple stain widening on the delicate green silk, and then looked up furiously, straight into Jake's dark eyes.

'How could you?' she gasped, grabbing at a box of tissues. 'Look what you've done!'

'I've done?' he drawled. 'I was under the impression you managed to pour that bottle over your skirt all by yourself.'

The varnish was running in little rivulets down her delicate green silk suit, spreading out and soaking through to her legs. She tore a wedge of tissue out of the box and swabbed desperately at the stain, not even really registering what she was doing through the turmoil in her brain.

He gazed at her expressionlessly. 'If you rub any harder, Sara,' he observed, 'you'll probably set your skirt on fire.'

Her hand lifted and she stared at him. Blue-black eyes gazed back. Eyes the colour of midnight. Then, almost as if it were an irrelevance, she suddenly remembered that in five minutes she was supposed to be leaving for the most important interview of her career.

Sara swallowed. 'My skirt's ruined,' she said. 'And it's all your fault.'

He gazed at her speculatively. 'Well, I wouldn't call it the end of the world,' he replied. 'Or do clothes really mean more to you than people?'

Sara clenched her jaw and counted to ten. 'Of course not,' she forced out. Truth to tell, her skirt had been almost the last thing on her mind. Jake and his brother, Jamie, were the only two subjects her mind could really focus on these days. But now Jamie was dead and she knew that Jake blamed her.

There was nothing she could do to show him how wrong he was. She had promised Jamie she would keep his secret. And now that he was dead, she would never break her word.

Silence stretched out between her and Jake once more, and she realized he was waiting for her to say something. Reply to some question. But what had he asked her? She shook her head. She simply had to get a grip on herself.

'This interview means a lot to me,' she said quickly, trying hard to sound brisk and business-like. 'Naturally I wanted to look my best.'

Jake smiled grimly and she felt a sudden flash of anger. Why did he have to look so cool and self-possessed even when he was wearing jeans and a white cotton shirt? His crisp dark hair could probably do with a trim, but his body was hard and well muscled. And there was a look in his eyes that meant few people ever tried to cross him.

She bit her lip and looked away. She had dressed with supreme care for that interview with French racing driver, Jean Paul Charpentier. But now with Jake's eyes on her, she knew that all her efforts had been to somehow impress the grim-looking man lounging on her desk.

Sleek blonde hair, carefully made-up face, beautifully cut silk suit. And all of them useless armour against Jake's corrosive gaze.

His eyes travelled down her body and back up again, missing nothing.

She felt the blood rush to her face, flooding down her neck and up into the roots of her hair. 'Stop looking at me like that,' she forced out, the colour deepening in her cheeks.

'Why?' he drawled. 'When it's obvious from the way you dress that you want everyone to stare at you. A walking fashion plate, who never has a hair out of place.' His lips twisted. 'Or a heart in the right place.'

'If you'll excuse me,' she grated, desperately trying to regain control, 'I have a job to go to. And even you would agree I can't go like this.'

Bits of tissue were sticking to her skirt like dandruff and all of a sudden she couldn't have cared less. She couldn't have made a worse impression on Jake if she had planned it out a month in advance.

Why had their conversation centred on her well-known weakness for clothes, when perhaps they could have come to some sort of an understanding about Jamie?

Sara grabbed her handbag and took a step backwards. 'This hasn't gone awfully well, has it?' she forced out. 'You think all I care about is my clothes, and I think...'

He leaned forward, interested, alert, but his tone was quiet and even. 'What, Sara? What do you think?'

It was the first time she had heard him speak gently to her for years and it was like a knife twisting in an old wound.

'Nothing,' she said quickly. 'It doesn't matter what I think.' She felt a sudden wave of panic at his closeness and looked desperately at the clock. 'All I know is I have exactly three minutes to persuade the fashion editor to lend me something else to wear before I leave to meet Paul Jean Parchentier.'

He stared at her reflectively, the ghost of a long-dead smile in his eyes. 'The man's name is Jean Paul Charpentier,' he corrected softly. 'I would have thought you would have got his name right even if you probably make up everything else about him.'

Sara compressed her lips. 'Of course I know his name,' she spat. 'I just . . .'

'Just what?' Jake probed all too innocently.

She opened her mouth and then closed it again. Why should she play into his hands by telling him how nervous he made her; how much even his presence affected her? 'Nothing,' she muttered.

Jake looked at her for a long moment and then shrugged. 'In any case, you won't be needing another skirt for the next few weeks at least. Not where you're going.'

She looked down at the ruined fabric and then back up at him, not really registering what he had said. 'Of course I'm going to need a skirt,' she said crossly. 'I've got to wear something.'

There was a look in his eyes that she couldn't read at all. But it sent a shiver down her spine all the same. She had been a fool to think that perhaps Jake had changed. It was obvious that raking over the past was not going to do either of them any good. So why couldn't he just leave her alone?

'I don't know why you're wasting your time even bothering to insult me,' she said tartly. 'You've made it perfectly plain you can't stand the sight of me. Ever since Jamie—'

'Ever since Jamie's death,' he cut in. 'And long before that, as you well know, I've thought of you as something pretty low in the scale of evolution, I must admit.' He leaned across her desk. 'But don't worry, sweetheart, I can always revise my opinion—downwards.'

Sara shivered. She had never really known why everything had seemed to go so horribly wrong between her and Jake. In the end, the best idea had seemed simply for her to avoid him over those long, long years. But now he was back, standing in front of her, gazing at her with those oh so deceptively soft eyes.

She glared at him. 'You know nothing about what happened between Jamie and me,' she said furiously. 'You weren't there and you just believe what you want to believe. And damn any evidence to the contrary.' She took another step backwards and stood as if poised to run. 'Now if you'll excuse me, Mr Armstrong, I have to go and speak sweetly to the fashion editor so I can keep my appointment with...' She paused and then carefully enunciated, 'Monsieur Charpentier.'

He sat on the corner of her desk and doodled on the back of a press release. 'Someone else is going to see your racing driver,' he said.

'What?' she gasped.

He put down the pen and looked up. ''Fraid so. And the features editor wants to see you,' he said mildly. 'Now.'

She clenched her jaw. 'You may be the son of the man who owns this newspaper,' she said coldly, 'but that doesn't mean you can play God with other people's lives.'

He gazed at her, the lazy arrogance in his eyes now all too obvious. 'Who says?'

She thought of five different suitably crushing retorts, but as he smiled down into her face, she pursed her lips instead and stalked off to the feature editor's office.

'Have you heard of a place called Bandhul?' Emma, Sara's boss, was sitting at her desk, looking as cool and immaculate as ever, and reading some agency copy.

Sara shook her head bewilderedly. 'Somewhere in India?'

'Near enough,' Emma sighed. 'It's up in the Himalayas, run by a few generals ever since a military coup twenty years ago. Now the people there are pushing for elections and there have been arrests and riots. I want a big colour piece, interviews, atmosphere, you know the sort of thing. Got your passport?'

Sara shut her mouth with a snap and tried to regain some of her self-control. She was horribly conscious of her ruined skirt and the look of disdainful amusement in Emma's eyes. 'Of course I haven't got my passport,' she bit out sarcastically, more rudely than she had meant. 'I was only going to the republic of South Kensington today.'

Emma glanced up at her. But her gaze was now as cold as the grey waters of the Thames outside her big office window. 'Well, you better get it,' she ordered. 'And then get round as quickly as possible to the Bandhul Embassy to collect your visas. The travel department has fixed it all up. Your plane leaves tonight.'

Sara sat down limply. 'Visas?' she repeated.

Emma stared at her impatiently. 'Well, you'll need two. One for you and one for Jake.'

The name was enough to jerk Sara suddenly back into life. 'Oh, no,' she said, standing up. 'Jake Armstrong? Now I know you're joking. Me go anywhere with him? You must be out of your mind.'

Her boss stared at her inquiringly. 'What's the matter with him? He's the best photographer in Fleet Street and he knows the country.'

'Yes,' snapped Sara. 'Maybe, but the last thing I need is Jake to hold my hand.'

'I doubt he'll be doing that,' remarked Emma coolly. 'This trip is strictly business, and from what I hear about the way you treated Jake's brother, I expect it to stay that way.'

Sara's jaw dropped. 'What exactly are you getting at?' she demanded.

'Nothing,' replied Emma. 'Except that you could say Jake and I have an...understanding. I'm not happy about this trip, especially from what I hear about the way you conduct your private life, but it seems I have no choice.'

Sara stared at her boss. Beautiful, calculating, ambitious—and by the angry look in her eyes, obviously obeying Jake's orders.

'I don't know what you've heard, and I don't care,' spat Sara. 'Because it's obviously all lies. But as far as Jake and I are concerned, you have absolutely nothing to worry about. In the first place, everyone knows I grew up with him as his stepsister, and I know him far too well to have any illusions of romance about him.'

Her boss opened her mouth, but Sara hadn't finished. 'And knowing you both as well as I do,' she said sweetly, 'I think you're extremely well suited.'

'Our relationship is none of your business,' Emma said coldly.

'It is when he uses it to force me into going to some rotten country in the middle of nowhere,' retorted Sara. 'Why don't you go with him, since you two have such a wonderful "understanding"?'

Emma stood up. 'My private life is not up for discussion,' she snapped. 'Especially not with you.'

Sara put a hand on her arm, her anger leaving as suddenly as it came. She had no right to take out her feelings on Emma. 'I don't know anything about your relationship,' she told her boss softly. 'But I do know lots about Jake. You know the best thing to do if you have a tiger by the tail?'

'What?' Emma asked involuntarily.

'Let go,' Sara replied simply.

The door swung open and both women looked up as Jake strolled in. It was odd how he suddenly made the room seem so much smaller, thought Sara, finding herself unable to stop staring at those eyes that were so dark they were almost black.

'Well, Sara,' he drawled, leaning on the desk and folding his arms, 'all ready to rough it?'

Emma looked from one to the other of them, uncertain of her ground, determined to be cheerful. 'Why don't you both have the same names?' she asked at last.

'I wanted to be independent,' replied Sara, turning with an effort back to Emma. 'To make my own way.'

'You always were the most pigheaded, stubborn woman I knew,' observed Jake.

'Our first meeting in how many years and already I'm smothering in compliments,' Sara said as sweetly as she could.

Jake's eyes flickered. 'Make the most of it,' he drawled. 'This is as nice as I get.'

Emma looked as though she had stepped into a mine-field. But she carried on bravely, as if impervious to the tension surging around her. 'Will I be seeing you later?' she asked Jake.

He shrugged, still staring at Sara. 'There's a lot to organize.' Then his voice gentled as he turned to Emma and added, 'I'll call you.'

She nodded and closed her handbag with a snap. Sara knew that Emma wanted her to leave her alone with Jake, but she stood her ground. She didn't feel any particular dislike for Emma, but she didn't see why she should make things any easier for Jake.

'I'll go, then,' remarked Emma at last, rather uncertainly. 'Seeing as I'm now at least ten minutes late for lunch with Jean Paul Charpentier.'

Sara bit her lip and glanced down at her ruined skirt. If only she had just got up and walked away when she saw Jake heading for her, then she would already be on her way to lunch with the so-called fabulous Frenchman. 'Have a nice time,' she muttered glumly.

Emma looked at her watch and smiled at Jake. 'Good luck.' And then glancing at Sara's ruined skirt, she added practically, 'You'll need it.'

The door closed behind her and Sara glared at Jake. 'You have no right to do this. Absolutely no right at all,' she forced out.

He sat down in Emma's chair and put his feet on the table. 'And what exactly have I done?' he inquired.

She lifted her hands and counted off on her fingers, 'Simply stopped me from getting the best interview I've had in months, and one I had to work like hell to set up. Using your influence to get me posted to this fly-blown job, where the best I can hope for is a bout of food poisoning. And making my life on this paper absolute misery.'

He shrugged. 'You can always leave.'

She stepped towards him, her hands clenched into fists. 'That's what you'd really like me to do, isn't it?' she snarled. 'You're blaming me for Jamie's death and now you want your pound of flesh.'

'I don't give a damn about you,' he said coldly. 'You treated my brother abominably, and now he's dead all you can think about is swanning around painting your nails and having lunch.'

The blood drained from her face. Did he really think that about her? 'That's simply not true,' she forced out. 'I work hard for this newspaper and I turn in good interviews with celebrities that other people couldn't get.

'But then,' she said sweetly, mimicking his tone, 'you spend so much time swanning off to take a few pictures here and there in whatever exotic place takes your fancy, that I don't really expect you to notice anything that goes on in this office.'

She could see a muscle jerking in his cheek now and she knew that she had been unfair. Jake was one of the best war photographers the Street had ever had, and the last place he had "swanned off" to was Bosnia. But then, when had Jake ever been fair to her?

He stared at her consideringly and then said softly, 'Oh, I notice what goes on here, Sara. And perhaps if we went through your expenses forms a little more carefully, you would end up paying us for the privilege of working here, however many so-called celebrities you manage to corner.'

'You can sneer,' she snapped. 'My job may not be a series of tough macho assignments like yours, but it does have one distinct advantage. It means I can keep out of your way.'

'You've been running for a long time,' remarked Jake. 'Don't you think it's time to stop?'

Sara swung away to the window and gazed out unseeingly at the sweeping view. 'I wasn't the one who ran out in the first place,' she said softly.

'A teenage indiscretion,' Jake replied coldly. 'I acted badly once towards you, and you've been punishing all of us ever since. Is that what this is all about?'

'A teenage indiscretion,' repeated Sara softly. She remembered that soft velvet night with sudden startling clarity and turned to face Jake. Is that what he had thought? 'Does it matter now?' she said wearily. 'Does any of it matter after all these years?'

His eyes hardened. 'Just the little matter of Jamie's death,' he said brutally. 'That's all that concerns me now.'

Colour flooded into her face. For one moment, she had forgotten about Jamie. Forgotten about the horror of those last few months. Jake must think she was completely heartless.

She opened her mouth to speak, but Jake was too quick for her. 'You're coming to Bandhul with me whether you like it or not,' he told her softly. 'And you'll tell me all I want to know. You'll also discover what hard work is like, for the first time probably. But if you fall down on the job there, you won't need to quit. I'll simply fire you.'

'I've never fallen down on any assignment,' spat Sara. 'But if you try anything, I'll—'

'Run to my father?' supplied Jake, his calm tones belying the dangerous light in his eyes. He shrugged. 'I wouldn't advise it. You may not know or care, but he's been quite ill recently. And his health wasn't improved by your antics with Jamie. He's stepping down next month, and I'm taking over the company.' He waited a few seconds for the news to sink in and then added silkily,

'If you have any complaints, I would advise you to follow the official procedure.'

'Official procedure,' Sara said feelingly. 'That's rich, coming from you. When did you ever follow official procedure?'

He stared gravely at her. 'I wasn't suggesting that I follow any procedure,' he said softly. 'But I'd like to see you try to come to grips with it. Petty of me, I know, but right now I'd welcome practically anything that would make your life more difficult.'

Sara swallowed. 'I tell you, I won't go on this trip. I'll save you the trouble and resign now.'

He gazed at her silently, and she was reminded of a top-class poker player deciding his next move. 'No, Sara, I don't think you will resign now. You can't afford to, for one thing. I mean—' he shrugged '—think of all the money you lavish on clothes...and nail varnish.'

She thought about her last letter from the bank and then looked him straight in the eyes. 'I'll easily get a job on another paper.'

'Will you?' he replied. 'Jobs are a bit limited on all papers these days, especially for people who could get the reputation for being ''difficult''.'

Sara's mouth dropped open. 'Even you wouldn't spread lies about me,' she whispered.

'Try me,' he said simply.

'Look,' she began. 'This is silly. I'm a features writer and I specialize in showbiz stuff. I'm simply not cut out for anything else. There must be hundreds of news reporters who'd give their right arms to do this job.'

'So Emma said,' he remarked. 'But we haven't got hundreds of reporters and the ones we have are all busy using their right arms to do their jobs properly.

'This story was my idea, I must admit. The whole situation in Bandhul could blow up, but it may turn out to be nothing. The news desk was reluctant in the extreme to send anyone of theirs who might end up out there for more than a few days. You, unfortunately, seem to be the only one available.'

'But it's ridiculous!' she exploded. 'I'm going to complain to the editor. I bet you never even consulted him at all.'

'Sam is on holiday,' said Jake, 'so you can't go crying to him. If I had my way, he'd be away permanently. He's the one who's supposed to run the whole editorial side of this newspaper and the only thing he ever does efficiently is collect his salary.'

Sara stared at him, anger and disbelief building up in her like a pressure cooker. 'But I've never been on a job like this in my life. I don't even really know where this place, Banjo, is,' she blazed.

'Bandhul,' he corrected, lifting his feet off the desk and standing up. 'And for the moment, you don't need to know. I'm sure the pilot of the aeroplane can find the way.'

She watched him head for the doorway, his tall, lean form filling up the door-frame. 'Why are you doing this?' she blurted out. 'What do you want from me?' He turned to face her and she rattled on desperately, 'I know you've used your influence to have me put on this job. Why? Emma's obviously less than happy about it.' She lifted her chin and looked at him defiantly. 'Why don't you take her instead and cement this wonderful "relationship" she told me about?'

He stepped towards her, his face grim, and she suddenly found herself clasping her hands nervously.

'Because I want to know exactly what happened to my brother, Sara. I don't want the lies that you've been feeding our family for the past six months while I've been away. Apparently, every time they've tried to talk to you about it, you've given them nothing but half-truths and evasions.' He reached out and tipped up her chin. 'This trip seemed the perfect opportunity to get the truth from you. And believe me, I will have it before we return. All of it.'

She tried to struggle away, the effect of his stare like a torch in her face. 'I'm not going to tell you any more than I've already told your father,' she forced out. 'I can't.'

'Can't?' he said quietly. 'Or won't?'

She thought of Jamie and blinked back sudden tears. 'Your brother was ten times nicer than you,' she spat.

'Oh, I don't doubt it,' he replied gently. 'But then I've always been the black sheep of the family.'

She clenched her jaw and said nothing.

'However,' he continued, 'there is one heavy advantage in being the prodigal son. Having broken every rule in the book, no one notices after a while when you break a few more.'

'Like organizing this trip,' she muttered.

'Exactly,' he agreed.

She grasped his fingers and pulled them away from her face. 'I will speak to your father,' she said. 'He wouldn't want me to be put through this.'

His eyes hardened. 'My father needs complete rest and quiet if he is to recover from his heart attack. So if you go anywhere near him or try to contact him in any way, I'll make sure you get sent somewhere that will make Bandhul look like an afternoon's shopping in Knightsbridge.'

Sara closed her eyes and breathed in as deeply as she could. She was not going to be riled by this man. She opened her eyes to find him still staring at her. 'For somebody who became a war photographer because he couldn't face becoming an arrogant old tycoon like his father, you're certainly following in his footsteps with a vengeance,' she said coldly.

His lips twisted. 'It's amazing what you can learn when you have to.'

'What stage are you at now?' she demanded. 'Intermediate bullying?'

He stepped towards her. 'Oh, I passed that stage long ago,' he said softly, trailing a lazy finger down her cheek. 'Now, I'm just catching up on demanding with menaces.' His finger stopped at her jawline and he looked right down into her eyes. 'It's amazing that one so beautiful as you can conceal such a rotten core,' he said softly.

She wanted to break away, to slap him in the face and just walk out. But something in his face stopped her. For reasons she didn't want to admit even to herself, she wanted this man to think well of her. To realize that she was not the heartless liar that he thought her.

'One day,' she whispered, 'you'll apologize to me for all this.'

His hand dropped from her face. 'I doubt it.'

'I tell you, I don't know anything!' she burst out.

He reached for the door handle and turned back to stare coldly at her. 'You know more than you're telling, Sara Thornton. And I mean to know every last bit of it.'

CHAPTER TWO

SARA shut her last suitcase with a snap and struggled with it to the hall of her tiny flat. If she was going to have to go to this blasted back-of-beyond country, then at least no one would be able to accuse her of not being prepared.

A picture of Jake's mocking face floated into her mind, and she muttered evilly under her breath. She simply wasn't going to fall down on this job.

It was obvious he thought little of her talents, and even less of her character, but if he expected to spend his time grilling her about Jamie, she would show him.

She would turn in the best damn piece she possibly could. And then she would resign and go somewhere where she would never have to see Jake again. After all, that was what they both wanted, wasn't it?

She clapped her hand to her head. Her passport. She had forgotten her passport and now she simply couldn't remember where she had put it. Swearing aloud, she began to ransack her flat, the shrilling of her front doorbell doing nothing to ease her panic.

'Don't tell me. This isn't your flat. You're simply an extremely untidy cat burglar in your spare time.'

Sara whirled around, holding aloft some rather scanty underwear she had just found. 'Jake!' she yelped.

He boosted himself off the door jamb. 'Your door was ajar so I just let myself in.' He nodded at the lingerie. 'Very fetching. But not exactly practical.'

Sara could feel herself flame up to the roots of her hair. She hurriedly stuffed the delicate silk back in a drawer. 'I was looking for my passport,' she said breathlessly.

'Passport to what?' he said sardonically. 'A good time?' She banged the drawer shut and turned to face him. But before she could speak, he added, 'So far this week, my office has had four phone calls from some creep called Gerry asking for you about a personal matter.'

'So?' she said defiantly.

'So I'd prefer it, if you don't mind,' he said with searing politeness, 'if you made sure your private phone calls went to the correct extension—or even better, that you dealt with them at home.'

'I'm sorry,' she said stiffly. 'I don't know what the operator was playing at. I'll make sure it doesn't happen again.'

He nodded slowly, looking around her flat, his eyes missing nothing.

Her hackles rose. 'We don't have to go on this trip, you know,' she burst out. 'If you dislike me so much, it might be better if we just called it a day now.'

He stepped up to her. 'Maybe,' he said softly. 'But we're both in the same boat, Sara.'

'Except that you're on the bridge, and I'm somewhere down below in the bilges, or whatever you call it,' she retorted bitterly.

He smiled at her. 'How well you put things.' Then turning away from her, he sighed. 'We avoided each other for so many years after what happened that summer,' he began. 'I was so angry with you at the time—'

'Angry with me?' Sara broke in, her words vibrating with disbelief.

He looked at her, his eyes glinting in the afternoon sunlight. 'When I got to Australia, the first thing I did was get extra work so I could afford to send you that

plane ticket. And all I got in return was the same ticket
torn into tiny pieces. Not even a message. That was a
pretty cruel thing to do, Sara, even for you.'

She stared at him, trying hard to take in what he was
saying. 'I didn't get any ticket,' she whispered.

His lips twisted. 'I wish I could believe you,' he replied grimly.

'No, but—' she began again.

He lifted his hands wearily. 'Save it, Sara. It was a
long time ago, and after what happened to Jamie, I just
don't care anymore. I don't even like the little I know
of you now, and ordinarily you would be my last choice
as a reporter for the Bandhul job. But—'

'You are so unbelievably arrogant, aren't you?' she
broke in, her shock at what he had told her sparking
into anger. 'If you were just a normal photographer instead of the up-and-coming owner of a newspaper, you
wouldn't have any choice in who was going with you.
After all,' she swept on, 'what do photographers know
about journalism? They can't even spell.'

Jake looked at her sardonically. 'Well, that will make
two of us, won't it?' he said softly. 'Although, from
what I've had the misfortune to read of your copy, I
was under the distinct impression that you were trying
to write the showbiz column in Esperanto.'

Sara clenched her jaw. She was simply not going to
rise to his bait. She watched tensely as he began to prowl
around the room and then her heart seemed to stop as
he stooped to pick up a photograph from a chest, his
face darkening as he studied it.

'Put that down,' she said as firmly as she could.

He gazed from the picture to her. 'I took this shot of
Jamie,' he said coldly. 'Where did you get it?'

'Your father gave it to me,' she muttered.

'It was in my room,' he said. 'You took it, didn't you?
While I was on my last assignment?'

Sara swallowed but said nothing.

'Didn't you?' he demanded.

She nodded and bit her lip. 'I guess I just didn't think
you'd miss it,' she said in a low voice.

He gave her one burning look and then turned the
frame over and snapped back the catches, easing out the
photo.

'What are you doing?' she cried, suddenly galvanized
by the realization of what was happening. 'Stop it!' She
launched herself at him, reaching for the little glossy
snapshot, the only memory she had now of Jamie, but
he caught her outstretched wrist with one hand and put
the photo into his shirt pocket. 'It's my photograph!'
she cried, beating his chest with her free hand until that,
too, was enclosed by his strong brown fingers.

'You stole it,' grated Jake, drawing her more tightly
towards him. 'And he was my brother. It's obvious now
that you never cared much for him alive, so why should
you want his picture after he's dead?'

'No wonder he hated you!' she spat, struggling use-
lessly to free herself from his iron grip.

And then as the enormity of what she had said sank
in, she stopped and looked horrified up into his eyes,
only inches from her own.

There was silence in the room now, so silent she could
hear her own breathing, and then even that caught in
her throat at his expression. 'I . . . I shouldn't have said
that,' she gasped as he bent his head to hers. 'I—' But
whatever she had been going to say was stopped by his
mouth on hers. Hard and bruising and insistent. Desperately she struggled against him, but as the pressure
of his mouth gentled, her hands stilled and she began
responding to him with a hunger she could not deny.

This was not how it should be, a small, lonely voice in her brain told her. Jake should repel her, not wake up emotions in her body that were best left undisturbed. Her hand crept up to caress his neck, her fingers searching into his thick, crisp hair, but suddenly he had pushed her away, a muscle pounding in his cheek. 'Very good,' he drawled, breathing deeply. 'But I don't think I'm ready to fall into the same trap again.'

Sara stared at him numbly, lifting trembling fingers to her lips. 'It was you who started this,' she said in a low voice. 'Don't try to pin the blame for your behaviour on me.'

He buttoned his shirt pocket, lightly smoothing his hand over the rectangular outline of the photo inside. 'I apologize,' he said formally, staring at her without any expression at all on his face.

'You don't mean a word of that,' Sara replied bitterly.

'No,' he agreed, 'I don't. But then, I don't believe you're really very upset. From what I've heard, it would take more than an unwanted kiss to pierce your armour-plated façade.'

'Jake,' she pleaded, 'don't. We were good friends once.'

'Is that what you call it?' he asked coldly. 'We were lovers, Sara. And you seemed so innocent, so trusting— so different from the real you. The woman who drove my brother to his death.'

Jake's lips twisted as he looked down at her.

'The Italians say a woman is better than a man at two things—love and revenge.' He shook his head slowly. 'You don't know the meaning of the first word, Sara. But I mean to teach you all about the second one.'

She swallowed. 'Please, Jake. This is madness.' She stared at him pleadingly, her hands clenched. 'You can't think this way about me. You can't... You've got completely the wrong picture. We have to talk. I . . .' She looked up at his grim features and her words trailed away.

'Oh, we'll talk,' he replied. 'But you can cut out all this hearts-and-flowers stuff. I'm not interested. It's all a front with you, Sara. You're just out for what you can get, and damn anyone who can't keep up.'

'Jake—' she began.

But he carried on remorselessly. 'Beggars can't be choosers in our job, Sara. You don't want to come with me to Bandhul, and if I'm honest I'd rather take a sackful of snakes. But you won't be able to hide from me there and I want to know about Jamie.

'This assignment will probably be my last job before I start taking over from my father. He can't wait much longer for the answers to Jamie's death. He's a tough old guy, but what with the heart attack, as well, it really knocked him for six. If you had any decency, you'd save us all a lot of heartache and just come clean now.'

Sara sat down limply on the sofa and closed her eyes as if that would blot out the horror of Jamie's death. 'I haven't got anything further to add to what I said at the inquest,' she whispered.

She opened her eyes to see Jake staring bitterly at her. 'We'll see,' he said grimly. 'We'll see.'

Sara opened her handbag to get a tissue and her fingers curled around her missing passport. She stood abruptly, snapping her bag shut. 'Let's get one thing straight,' she said as bravely as she could. 'I'm not the kind of person you think I am. And maybe this trip will show you that. But whatever you think, and whatever you do, I'm being sent there to do a job and I'm going to do it as well as I can.' She paused and swallowed. 'With or without your help.'

Was that a faint look of respect in Jake's eyes? she wondered. Or, she thought bitterly, was it just a trick of the light?

He looked at her consideringly. 'That was a pretty good speech, Sara,' he said, nodding. 'I just wish I could believe you.'

She bit her lip. 'I remember when you were a nice person to know,' she said softly, without even thinking of what she was saying. 'What happened?'

'At least I didn't lose my identity,' he grated. 'I can still be "nice", as you so charmingly put it, to people I like. But you...'

Sara swallowed and lifted her chin. 'I what?' she demanded. 'Go on, say it.'

He shook his head and turned away from her abruptly. 'As long as I live, I'll never understand you, Sara,' he said at last. 'You have got to be the most shallow, vain and silly person I know. And yet occasionally, just very occasionally, like now, you stand up and challenge the whole world to sock you on the chin.'

Sara stared at his back, the strong, wide shoulders tapering into a narrow waist, and, in a fit of desperation, tugged him by the elbow. 'Look at me, Jake,' she pleaded.

He turned and stared at her. 'What?' he demanded quietly. 'What can you possibly say to me now, after all that has happened?'

She swallowed and looked him straight in the eye. 'I might be silly,' she said at last. 'If believing in the things you're told by people you love is silly, then I'm probably the most foolish person on the planet. Vain—' she shrugged '—yes, probably I'm vain. I like to look good because then it's one less thing people can criticize you for.' Her lips twisted. 'Of course, I can't really win there, because if I didn't dress up, I'd just be accused of not caring about my appearance.'

She made a little helpless gesture with her hands. 'But I'm not shallow, Jake. Never that. I guess celebrity showbiz stuff is a rather silly, shallow job compared to yours, and some of the outward ridiculousness of it all rubs off, but deep down, in here—' she thumped her chest '—I'm not shallow.'

She saw the impatience in his eyes and rushed on. 'I know you don't believe a word I say, and I can't help that. But I've never been knowingly cruel to anyone in my life. I didn't drive Jamie to his death. I didn't—'

'So you say,' Jake ground out harshly. 'But you weren't exactly helpful and forthcoming about the time leading up to his death. Actions speak louder than words, Sara. And yours positively shout about how badly you behaved.'

Her eyes narrowed. 'You weren't there,' she snapped. 'So how can you judge? Jamie needed you and you weren't there, and that's an end to it.'

He glared at her. 'So you're blaming me now, is that it? Trying to offload your guilt on me?'

Sara thumped her fist on the chest of drawers. 'Are you always this arrogant these days?' she yelled.

He smiled down at her. But it wasn't a particularly comforting smile. 'Oh, I can be much worse than this, Sara, as I expect you'll find out.'

She stalked into the hall. 'These are my suitcases,' she said coldly.

He looked at them in surprise. 'All of them?' It was probably the first time she had ever seen him truly nonplussed.

'Of course all of them,' she retorted. 'I'm the vainest person you know, remember? And besides, I haven't the faintest idea what this country is going to be like and I want to be prepared for any eventuality.'

'We're not spending the rest of our lives in Bandhul,' he said impatiently. 'Just a week or so.'

She held her head high, hating him for embarrassing her. 'I've only packed what I consider to be essentials,' she said coldly. 'Nightclothes, warm clothes, rain wear, formal dress, towels—'

'Which one's the lightest?' he cut in. Numbly she pointed at the smallest and he held it out to her. 'You take it,' he ordered. 'I'll deal with the rest.'

Sara got into the cab and began talking to the driver, purposely ignoring Jake. But she turned to him when he got in beside her. 'Did you put my cases in the boot?' she demanded.

'What cases?' he drawled.

'The ones you were going to bring out,' she said exasperatedly.

'I didn't say I was going to bring them,' he replied. 'I said I'd deal with them, so I left them where they were. It seemed the most logical solution.'

'You did what?' she screeched.

'Think of all the money you'll save on excess baggage fees,' he pointed out.

Her mouth opened. 'But my clothes—'

'Were completely unsuitable,' he said. 'You'll have to get some proper kit. We're going to one of the most uncomfortable places in the world, not a cocktail party.' Jake opened the glass partition behind the driver's head. 'White's camping shop in Oxford Street,' he said. 'And then the Bandhul Embassy, off Portman Square.'

'A camping shop?' echoed Sara, suddenly jerked back in her seat as the driver set off. 'Don't tell me we'll be staying in a tent?'

'No. But you'll need a sleeping-bag, proper boots and warm clothing.' He looked down at her and smiled grimly. 'Why so depressed? I thought you liked shopping. And they have some very fetching ranges of thermal underwear these days, so I'm told.'

Sara glared at him and thought longingly of everything she had packed. Blast Jake Armstrong and his all-consuming arrogance. One thing was for certain. She would get even with him, one way or another, before this trip was over.

She waited in the taxi for what seemed an age while Jake went into the embassy for their visas. For some reason, he had seemed reluctant for her to accompany him, and not wishing to have another row over something so trivial, she had decided to let him get on with it his way.

She looked at the small mountain of bags on the floor of the taxi. Thick, practical socks in sludge green and a nylon jacket and over-trousers poked through the top of one package. Was she really going to wear all that stuff? And what did she want with a rucksack?

Rain slid down the cab windows and blurred Jake's returning form, but she could have sworn there was a merest hint of a smile on his normally grim features.

He pulled the door open and clambered inside as the taxi jolted off on the trip to the airport.

Sara gazed at the raindrops trickling down his face and then rummaged in her bag. 'Here,' she offered tentatively, holding out a paper hanky. 'Go on. It's perfectly clean.'

He hesitated and then took it. 'Thanks,' he said, a small note of surprise in his voice.

'It's all right,' she said with a shrug. 'Even vain, silly and shallow people like me have their good points.'

He stopped wiping his face and looked at her, the ghost of a laugh in his eyes. 'Giving me a crumpled tissue hardly puts you in the Mother Theresa class, Sara,' he said.

'At least I haven't asked for it back,' she retorted.

'True,' he said, nodding. 'But then maybe you're just getting soft in your old age.'

'I'm twenty-five,' she said tartly. 'As well you know, considering I was five years old the day Pa brought me to the house and it was your twelfth birthday. You gave me three slices of cake and then I burst into tears because I couldn't eat my tea.'

There was a small silence. 'Pa,' Jake said quietly at last. 'I'd forgotten you called him that.'

Sara looked away quickly. 'How is he?' she asked abruptly.

Jake shrugged. 'As well as can be expected, considering everything that's happened.'

She pushed herself more deeply into the corner of the taxi's hard leather seat, as if even an inch more of distance between them would somehow count, and gazed covertly at Jake.

From that stilted exchange of phrases, they could almost be distant relatives swapping small talk, instead of…what? What were they after all this time? Enemies? Old lovers? Brother and sister? Perhaps that was why she had spent so long avoiding him. Because she couldn't bear to find out once and for all that he truly disliked her.

Sara had always wanted to work on newspapers. As she'd been brought up in the Armstrong household, it would have been considered rather odd if she hadn't. But after Jake and she… She shook her head and bit her lip. Even now she didn't want to think about it. After what had

happened, she had deliberately chosen a branch of
journalism that she knew he had no interest in. It had
still been rather tricky, in the small world of national
newspapers, to keep out of his way, but she had managed
it.

She had only gone back to *The Globe* because she
wanted to please Pa. And then all that business with
Jamie had blown up and now here she was planning to
spend the next few days being closer to Jake than she
had been for years. Nearly eight long years.

'What are you thinking?'

She jerked towards Jake as if he had woken her up.
'Hmm?' she said confusedly. 'Oh, nothing much. Just
about how things turn out. You know.'

'No, I don't know,' he said evenly. 'Tell me.'

She compressed her lips in sudden anger. Why did he
have to put her through all this? Why couldn't he just
trust her instead of continually questioning her and expecting the worst?

'I was thinking how rotten you were to me when you
were fifteen and I was eight,' she lied at last.

'I was never that rotten to you,' he said softly.

'Well, I suppose you did stop Jamie from amputating
my teddy bear's right leg,' she conceded. 'Although I
don't think he ever forgave you. He said he had to
practise on something if he was going to grow up to be
a world-famous surgeon. I suppose it was just lucky for
poor old teddy that you were around that day.'

She looked at Jake, but the hopeful smile died on her
face. Why on earth had she brought up that memory
out of all the ones of their childhood? The softening
lines in Jake's face hardened. 'Jamie always did have
high hopes for the future,' he said shortly, turning away
from her.

*   *   *

Sara looked down at the brown, wrinkled country way below her and sighed. This had been the longest trip she'd ever made, and the pressurized atmosphere of the succeeding jets they had taken was beginning to wear her down. She would be glad to breathe fresh air again— especially for more than just an hour or two on a stop- over, as they had been doing.

She stole a look at Jake asleep next to her and felt unreasonable annoyance that he looked so calm and self-assured even when he was unconscious. Even his mouth, with those full, generous lips, remained closed, unlike the businessman across the aisle who had snored in fits and starts for two hours before getting off at their last stop in Islamabad.

'Jake,' she whispered.

No reply.

She tugged his sleeve. 'Jake, wake up. I'm sure we're nearly there.'

His eyes opened and he stared at her sleepily. She had often thought how unfair it was that someone she had so much cause to dislike should be the most handsome man she had ever seen. And now, with his guard down, he reminded her even more painfully of that stupid way he had affected her as a teenager.

'You're thinking secret thoughts again,' he said softly.

She shook her head. 'Nothing of the sort,' she said abruptly.

He shot her a disbelieving glance and sat up, leaning across her to look out of the Perspex window. He was so close that she could breathe in his clean male smell and her senses reeled with the memories it evoked. She had forgotten how his hair curled on the back of his neck, and with an effort she stopped herself from reaching out to touch it.

'Well, those are the Himalayas, all right,' he said, withdrawing back into his own seat.

'But they're so brown!' she protested more vehemently than she had meant. Damn the way he was affecting her. She breathed deeply and forced herself to look him straight in the eyes. 'I thought they'd be all green with snowy tops.'

His lips twisted. 'And maybe a couple of Abominable Snowmen waving from the summit of Everest?' he suggested.

Sara coloured. 'Don't make fun of me,' she snapped, her eyes dropping.

'Why not?' he said, shrugging. 'It annoys you and amuses me.'

Desperate not to catch his eye, she looked out of the window again.

'It's no good, Sara,' he said at last. 'You can't sulk forever.'

'I am not sulking,' she grated.

'Yes, you are,' he drawled. 'It's obvious from your shoulders.'

She turned round furiously. 'Stop it, Jake. You've told me you don't like me. You've told me how much you despise me. So why—'

'Make fun of you?' he supplied.

She nodded tightly and he reached out and touched a strand of her hair. She could almost feel the electricity of his touch travel down it and she jerked away. His eyes gleamed. 'I've never known anyone who so hated to be laughed at,' he said softly.

'Try looking in the mirror,' she grated.

His expression hardened. 'I don't mind what I see when I look at my reflection,' he replied. 'But I'm not certain I could look myself in the eye if I were you.'

'I have done nothing to be ashamed of,' she spat.

'That rather remains to be seen, don't you think?' he said silkily.

'Not by you,' she retorted.

He sighed. 'It doesn't matter how you try to avoid the issue of what exactly you did do, Sara,' he said at last. 'In the end, you and I both know that you'll tell me everything.'

'Don't count on it,' she said coldly, trying desperately to keep her composure. Changing the subject abruptly, she demanded, 'What were you saying about the Himalayas?'

He gazed at her for a long moment and she looked away first. How was she ever going to get through this trip? But when he spoke he was perfectly serious. 'Nothing, really. Except that you won't see Everest from here. That's miles away near Kathmandu.'

'And Bandhul?'

'That's on a sort of plateau, about twelve thousand feet up. It's very dry and the air is very thin, and at this time of year, in March, there isn't a great deal of lushness.'

'Well, what on earth is there?' she demanded.

He shrugged. 'Difficult to explain,' he said at last. 'But I've been here twice before, and the place gets to you. There's a sort of magical innocence about the people that won't let you go.'

'What about the political situation?' she asked. 'What's the best way to proceed? Do you think it's worth asking those generals you talked about for an interview?'

'Only if you want to end up in jail,' he said. 'We're going to have to be extremely discreet if we're going to get anywhere.'

Sara looked sharply at him, but he had turned away and was beckoning a stewardess. There was something in his tone that was beginning to ring very loud danger bells all through her brain.

'Jake,' she began after the stewardess had gone, 'why didn't you tell me all this before?'

'All what?' he said innocently.

'You know perfectly well what I mean,' she said crossly. 'All this stuff about the need for discretion. I thought we were going on a perfectly straightforward job.'

He smiled wryly at her. 'Unfortunately, Sara, I've come to find out that countries on the brink of revolution, or at least outright rebellion, are never particularly straightforward jobs.'

She pressed her lips together at his light, mocking tones. He was right, of course. She should have listened more carefully when Emma was outlining what she wanted. But then, she had had something else on her mind at the time: Jake.

'I still think you should have been more open and informative,' she said at last.

'You sound like one of those pamphlets that the personnel department occasionally distributes on the secrets of happy man-management,' he said in a bored tone.

'Yes, well,' she replied caustically, 'how would you know? You've obviously never read them.'

He looked at her, his expression completely deadpan. 'If you were one-tenth as good an operator as you keep telling everyone you are, Sara, you would have gone to the cuttings library at work and read up on all this stuff.'

'I didn't get a chance,' she protested. 'And you know it.'

'Maybe you shouldn't have wasted all those hours packing,' he said smoothly.

The memory of that brief scuffle at the airport came back with all too blinding clarity. 'Maybe I didn't expect you to up-end my case all over the floor by the check-in desk and do my repacking for me,' she said icily.

He shrugged. 'Somebody had to,' he replied coolly. 'If I had trusted it to you, you would have left all your new stuff in the ladies' somewhere, just out of some twisted idea of spiting me.'

Sara coloured hotly. 'That's not true!' she retorted, unable to meet his eye.

'Isn't it?' he said blandly, tipping up her chin and holding her gaze.

She pulled away and looked out of the window. 'Some of those clothes you threw in that airport bin cost me an arm and a leg. And the suitcase alone was worth a small fortune. It was just silliness to dump them like that. Especially for the sake of some really ugly clothes and a rucksack I wouldn't want to be seen dead with.'

'I take it all back about your being vain,' Jake remarked idly. 'You're obviously the most self-effacing person in this part of the universe, with absolutely no problems about your self-image at all.'

Sara's face flushed once more. She had fallen right into that one. 'When I need a psychiatrist, I'll fly to Vienna, thank you,' she said tightly. 'Not to the back of beyond with someone whose ego is so large it has to be checked in as excess baggage.'

Jake's eyes glinted down at her. 'My ego may be large,' he conceded, 'but it won't get as much in the way as a trunkful of towels and formal wear.'

'The only thing your ego does for you is encourage you to demand exorbitant salaries from trusting newspaper editors,' spat Sara. 'Which allow you to swank around the world and do terribly macho things like drinking beer straight from the bottle.'

He was grinning outright at her now. 'You must tell me the names of some of these editors,' he said interestedly. 'A trusting one who hands out huge chunks of dosh for me to do nothing much is a person I would really like to meet.'

'I'd rather you met with a really sticky end,' she retorted.

Jake shook his head. 'Are you going to be like this all the time?' he asked softly.

'Like what?' she demanded.

'Prickly and quick to take offence,' he replied.

Her mouth dropped open. 'I wasn't prickly until you started winding me up,' she replied. 'It just so happens that I was rather fond of some of those clothes you threw away. And I hate it when you get on that high horse of yours and start telling me what to do.'

'We were late for our flight, remember?' Jake said softly. 'In any case, when you wake up shivering in the middle of a cold Bandhul night, you'll thank me that you've got something practical you can put on to warm yourself up.'

Sara looked at him with some asperity. 'If it gets cold, I shall merely turn up the radiator in my hotel bedroom like any sensible person would.'

He nodded slowly and thoughtfully, a glint in his eyes that she couldn't quite place. 'Yes, of course,' he agreed. 'That radiator in your hotel bedroom. How silly of me not to realize that you have probably already sent your personal plumber ahead, with strict instructions on how to introduce full gas central heating to the hotel of your choice.'

Sara's jaw dropped. 'You mean there's no heating out there?' she said at last.

Jake shrugged. 'Not much. They have fires, of course. But when people get cold they just tend to put on warm clothes. I suppose you could call it their version of formal evening wear.'

The dripping sarcasm in his words made her eyes snap. 'I could kick you right now, Jake Armstrong,' she snarled.

'Oh, I wouldn't do that,' he drawled. 'I might just kick you right back.'

'You're no gentleman, are you?' she said coldly.

'No,' he agreed. 'But then, you're no lady, either.'

Sara was still fuming as they got off the jet and trailed into the crumbling building that passed for customs control. Jake had been right; the air was thin and no matter how much she breathed in, she just couldn't seem to get enough.

Jake put his hand under her arm. 'Relax,' he said softly. 'Just take deep breaths. You soon get used to it, you'll see.'

She opened her mouth to say something smart, but thought better of it. Truth to tell, she felt completely floored by the jet lag and the gasping effect of being at such a high altitude. If she was going to be honest with herself, she was glad of his support. Not that she had to tell him that.

The customs official studied their passports and then looked at Jake. 'Purpose of visit?'

'Pleasure,' Jake replied.

The official smiled and then, studying their visas once more, brightened perceptibly and beamed widely at Sara. 'May I wish you a very pleasant honeymoon,' he said.

CHAPTER THREE

'HONEYMOON!' snarled Sara under her breath as Jake hurried her to the exit doors. 'What do you mean, I'm on honeymoon with you? I'd rather have a romantic weekend with a rattlesnake.'

'Yes, well,' said Jake, shrugging, 'you'd probably be more at home with one, I agree. But if I were you, I'd get out of earshot of any of those guards before you start arguing the toss about our marital status.'

He put his hand under her arm and, smiling in the friendliest fashion at two rather inscrutable-looking guards, guided her outside.

The bright sunshine hit her first, and then as she took in her surroundings she stood stock-still. Jake, his hand dropping from her arm, stopped, too, and looked down at her. 'What's the matter?' he asked. As he looked more closely at her face, his tone gentled. 'Sara? Are you all right?'

She shook her head speechlessly and then turned to him, desperately trying to keep the quaver out of her voice.

'Jake?' she said hesitantly.

He gazed at her, his expression softening. 'What is it?'

She swallowed and looked around once more at what was confronting her. 'Where the hell are we, Jake?' His eyes followed her gaze as it travelled over a flat, grey, rocky valley surrounded on all sides by soaring mountains, all shining white in the blinding sunshine. 'It's as if we're at the bottom of a volcano,' she whispered.

'We're on the only flat bit that was long enough to build an airstrip,' explained Jake. 'But it's not at the bottom of anything. It's practically on the roof of the world.'

She looked back at the shabby little hut they had just come from and then at the three or four broken-down buses parked in front of them. There seemed to be nothing else.

In the almost eerie silence it was as though she and Jake were suddenly the only two people on the planet. Instinctively she reached for his arm, her fingers curling around his wrist. And then looking up at him once more, the hard lines of his face accentuated in the harsh light, she remembered why she was in this God-forsaken place and her hand dropped to her side. It was ridiculous to think she could expect even simple human comfort from Jake.

'What now?' she inquired as calmly as she could.

He turned to her and smiled grimly. 'We get a taxi, of course. What else?'

'What else indeed?' she muttered. 'Apart from a few explanations, of course.' But Jake was already several strides ahead and she stumbled hurriedly along in his wake, bitterly regretting the rebelliousness that had made her decide to keep on her stilettos. It looked like she was going to have to wear those boots he had bought her after all.

The taxi turned out to be a modern-looking Jeep, and Sara sank thankfully into its comfortable back seat. To her surprise, Jake put his arm round her when he got in beside her, and smiled lovingly into her face. 'Never mind, darling, we'll soon be there.'

She looked up at him in astonishment, but the sharp retort she had been going to make died on her lips at the warning look on his face and the way he fractionally cocked his eyes at the driver and the man in uniform sitting beside him in the front.

'Not soon enough for me,' she said feelingly as Jake's arm slid more possessively around her shoulders and pulled her close. How dare he get her into this mess?

She struggled ineffectually to shrug off his arm, but then as she saw the guard's eyes watching her in the rear-view mirror, she stopped and instead put her hand out to touch Jake's face.

His fingers came up to enclose hers and he turned to look down at her. 'What?' he said softly, his expression guarded at her sudden seeming affection.

'Nothing,' she whispered back. 'I just wanted to see if it was true that these days you were completely made of ice.'

'This is it,' said Jake. 'Bandhul City limits.'

Sara opened her eyes from the uneasy doze she had fallen into and looked about with interest. Then she glanced, bewildered, at Jake. 'I don't understand,' she said. 'Was that a joke?'

He shook his head. 'It's not exactly Kensington High Street, I agree, but here we are.'

Sara looked at the squat grey buildings on either side of the road, and the crowds of people everywhere. They looked with keen interest at the Jeep, with shuttered faces at the driver and guard, but with wide-open smiles at Sara and Jake. The noise and the smells and the clear, bright light were almost overwhelming, and Sara pressed her hands to her forehead. She was beginning to have the mother and father of all headaches.

The crowds grew more congested as the Jeep progressed towards the centre, finally pulling off into what was obviously a depot. 'This is where the airport truck will bring our luggage this evening,' explained Jake.

'What about our hotel?' Sara asked faintly. 'Do they really have such things in this town?'

'Oh, yes.' Jake smiled sardonically. 'They really do. Come on.' And shouldering his bag, he set off. Sara took one despairing look at her shoes, now cruelly biting her feet, and trailed, exhausted, after him.

'I don't understand all this business with the guard,' she said when she finally caught with him. 'If he was so keen to escort us all the way here, why isn't he with us now?'

'Gone off duty, I expect.' Jake shrugged.

'Very funny,' replied Sara.

He cocked a glance at her. 'I meant it,' he said easily. 'There are plenty of people in this city who will keep an eye on what we get up to. As westerners, we're not exactly going to melt into the background after all.'

'Then how are we going to do our job?' demanded Sara. 'It's going to be impossible interviewing people about their views of the government if we are to be spied on at every turn.'

Jake stopped suddenly and Sara cannoned into him. 'Why do you think we're supposed to be on our honeymoon here?' he said softly, steadying her.

'Some sort of sick joke, I expect,' Sara replied witheringly.

His hand gripped her arm and he shook her slightly. 'Perhaps it's escaped your attention, Sara, but we're here on a job. Now would be a very good time for you to stop thinking about yourself and start trying to earn that vastly inflated salary of yours.'

'Pretending to be on honeymoon with you,' she observed searingly, 'is rather beyond the ordinary call of duty. And if you'd told me about this in London, you could have had my resignation there and then—even if you had fixed it for me to never work on any other newspaper ever again.'

Jake, his grip tightening on her arm, swung her to face him. 'Why do you think I didn't tell you?' he demanded. 'You're not going to resign until I'm finished with you, Sara. And you're not going to give me the run-around over Jamie that you've given everyone else.'

She glared at him. 'I'm not going to tell you anything,' she forced out. 'No matter how much you bully me.'

His hand dropped from her elbow and she rubbed it with studied care. It was a childish gesture, especially as he had not hurt her at all, but she was too tired and disorientated to be reasonable.

'I don't want to bully you,' he said at last. 'You know I'm not that kind of a person.'

'Do I?' she flared. 'Why should I know what kind of person you are, Jake, when we've managed to avoid each other for nearly eight years?'

He stared blackly at her. 'You're the one who has always avoided me,' he grated. 'And I guess, for several stupid reasons, I've let you. But that's all over now.' He sighed and rubbed a weary hand over his face. 'If I'm honest, I suppose I had hoped to appeal to some sense of honour and decency that you might still have tucked away somewhere.'

Sara glanced at him anew, startled by the sudden weariness in his tone. 'I'm sorry, Jake,' she whispered at last. 'I wish you could believe me when I say I can't tell you about Jamie. But I just can't.'

His lips tightened and the moment, when perhaps she could have told him everything, was over. 'We'll see,' he said grimly. 'In the meantime, as far as this job is concerned, we are simply crazy foreigners who had come here on honeymoon because we thought it would be the most romantic place on earth.

'Naturally we have eyes for nobody but ourselves, but there will be times when we'll want to go sightseeing and I'll be taking lots of pictures of my so-called darling wife against backgrounds that, of course, we are not to know are government installations.'

Sara nodded in unwilling admiration at his boldness, firmly closing her mind to their personal problems and focusing on what he was telling her. 'And then there's all that souvenir hunting we'll have to do in the market and anywhere else that takes our fancy,' she suggested. 'Will you be able to fix an interpreter? We could talk to an awful lot of people that way.'

Jake stared at her for a long moment. 'Trust you to bring shopping into it,' he said at last, his tone surprisingly mild.

'I'm an expert at it,' she said coolly. 'Remember? And there's certainly not going to be much else to do.'

The hotel, when they got to it, proved to be a long, three-storey whitewashed building with a big wooden door and charmingly painted shutters over the small, deep-set windows.

It was dark and cool inside after the harsh afternoon sunlight. Sara watched Jake go into a little office on the left and decided to go off on her own in search of the bar. Surely the hotel, dingy as it was, must have one.

She felt like ordering a gallon of sparkling mineral water, chinking with ice and so cold the glass would be misty with condensation. She'd make sure they put a thick slice of lemon in it, too; she could almost see it, bumping gently on the bubbles.

Her mouth watering, she pushed open the door nearest to her and stared aghast at its occupants.

'What's the matter?' said a voice she knew only too well. 'Don't tell me you're scared of a couple of yaks.'

'It's a stable,' said Sara wildly, turning to look Jake in the face. 'A stable in the middle of a hotel. I just don't believe it.'

'Best place for it,' replied Jake. 'Safe from thieves and keeps the upper floors warm. You see—they have got central heating after all.'

'Don't be ridiculous,' snapped Sara, suddenly to her astonishment close to tears. 'What do you think this is— the Middle Ages? Well, I've had just about enough of you and this crazy fly-blown place. Plus I don't care if I never see, or smell, another yak again. I'm going home.'

Jake put out a hand and drew her back. 'And just how do you think you're going to do that?'

She stared at him with angry eyes. 'Get a taxi to the airport, of course. What else?'

He shook his head slowly and then lifting his fingers from her arm gently stroked her cheek.

'Don't,' she bit out, shivering away from him.

'You can't go home,' he said softly. 'There are planes only twice a week. You'll have to wait at least another three days.'

'Which, I suppose, will give you plenty of time to bait me about Jamie,' she said bitterly.

His hand dropped to his side, his eyes hardening. 'Yes, it will, won't it?' he agreed in a harsh voice.

The hotel was built around a central courtyard, all the doors to the bedrooms opening on to wooden galleries running around it. Sets of steps, not much better than a ladder, connected each gallery.

'It's like workmen wandering around on scaffolding,' remarked Sara as she trudged along, clutching her handbag like an old friend and trying without much success to sound cool and composed. 'I'm surprised we don't have to wear hard hats and carry a shovel.'

'Only if you're going to the stable,' said Jake.

'Very funny,' she said under her breath, following him up the next flight of steps to the third floor.

Her jaw dropped when he opened the door to their room. 'The honeymoon suite, madam,' he announced with a flourish, motioning her in.

Sara's eyes took in the plain iron bedstead, a chair, a rickety table with a large Thermos and a couple of glasses perched on top of it, and . . . Her gaze swivelled around the whole of the room. 'Is this it?' she asked faintly.

Jake dumped his bag on the polished wooden floor. ''Fraid so,' he said.

She sat down with a bump on the bed. 'There aren't any duvets,' she said, looking at two rough brown blankets folded at the foot of the thin, hard mattress, which was covered in a coarse but clean linen sheet. 'Do you think room service . . .?' She looked into Jake's eyes and her voice trailed off. 'No,' she sighed, 'don't answer that. I get the picture.' Seeing his jaw tightening, she looked around and said brightly, 'Well, at least there are pillows.' She put her hand on one and recoiled hurriedly, glancing up at him. 'They're stuffed with grass, Jake.'

He nodded, his face expressionless. 'Look on the bright side, Sara. If you meet a hungry yak in the middle of the night, you'll have something to feed it with.'

Sara shot him a look that would have stripped paint and stalked over to the table, carrying her pillow.

'What are you doing?' he demanded as she emptied the stuffing over it.

'I'm just making absolutely certain I'm going to be resting my head on grass and nothing else,' she replied.

His lips suddenly twitched. 'You mean, you think there may be some exotic creepy-crawly curled up in there?'

She nodded. 'That's exactly what I mean,' she said firmly.

'You could always chuck the grass away and stuff the pillowcase with your clothes instead,' he suggested.

She looked up at him and then down once more at the sweet-smelling grass she had checked and was now busily stuffing back in the pillow. 'You must be joking,' she said, hoping her matter-of-fact tones would disguise the fear and resentment at her situation that were slowly building up in her. 'If I have to share that bed with you, I am going to be wearing every stitch of clothing I possess.'

'Sounds like the perfect honeymoon,' he remarked drily.

Sara looked at the charmingly painted beams in the low ceiling and then out of the window at the stunning view of the mountains. The room might be basic, but it was clean and blankets looked thick and soft. With the sleeping bags and everything else Jake had insisted on bringing, their stay here would be very comfortable. Physically, if not mentally. Not that she had admitted that to Jake.

She turned from the view to gaze at him, the top of his head brushing one of the beams. 'How exactly did you fix all this up, Jake? This place doesn't exactly conform to normal tourist standards, does it? Not by a long chalk.'

He gazed at her assessingly. 'Tourist groups are allowed here occasionally,' he said at last. 'They're mostly mountaineers or hillwalkers and they don't much mind roughing it. In fact, some people rather like it. Which is just as well, because this country is rather short on luxury.'

'You don't say,' muttered Sara.

But Jake ignored her and swept on, 'I have an ac-
quaintance in the Bandhul Embassy who, for a small
consideration and in the knowledge that he was helping
true love get off to the right start, agreed to regard us
as, what you might call, a small group.'

'A very small group,' Sara agreed coldly. 'And already
I can't stand the only other person in it.'

'Give it time,' Jake said with a glint in his eye. 'After
all,' he added smoothly, 'we have our whole lives to get
to know each other better.'

'I wouldn't give you five minutes,' she retorted.

'You have to give me at least three days,' he corrected
her.

Sara remembered the pillow in her arms and thumped
it back into shape. 'Don't remind me,' she snarled.

Jake sat on the mattress and looked at her. 'I must
admit you are taking this very well,' he remarked. 'I expected all sorts of tears and tantrums.'

'Did you?' she said bitterly. 'I'm not eight years old
any more, Jake. I'm a journalist, not a little girl crying
over her teddy bear.

'You walked out of my and Jamie's lives when we were
seventeen, and now you've come back, you think you
can just pick up where you last left off. A lot of water
has gone under the bridge since then. Maybe too much.'

Sara gazed up at him and shivered at the look in his
blue-black eyes. 'A very apt metaphor,' he grated. 'Considering how Jamie met his death.'

She swallowed. 'I had nothing to do with that. If you
had read up the report of the inquest in the papers, you
would have realized I wasn't even in the car at the time
it went into the river.'

'You were the last person to see him alive,' rasped
Jake. 'What did he say to you before he went careering

out of control on that road? Or more importantly,' he added menacingly, 'what did you say to him?'

'Nothing,' she forced out, adding suddenly in a low voice, 'I can't remember.'

He nodded slowly. 'Well, at least that's a start.'

'I don't know what you mean,' she snapped.

'From "nothing" to "I can't remember" is something of a leap, wouldn't you say?' he said silkily. 'All we have to do now is restore that obviously faulty memory of yours.'

Sara raked her hands nervously through her hair, its once-shiny strands now dust-coated from the trip in the Jeep.

'Look, Jake,' she began, 'I know you're angry with me—'

'Angry?' he said grimly. 'That must be the understatement of the year.'

She shook her head. 'No, please. Let me finish.'

He leaned back against the bed head, his hand resting easily on one upraised knee. Everything about him was relaxed and unhurried—only his hard expression gave any clues to his feelings. 'Go on, then,' he said at last. 'I'm listening.'

Sara's fingers curled around the edge of the table behind her and she drew a deep breath. 'It's no good, Jake. No matter how much you hound me about Jamie, I can't tell you any more than I already have.'

'Can't or won't?' he grated.

She lifted her chin and gazed at him directly. 'Let it go, Jake,' she said more calmly than she felt. 'Please. If only for Jamie's sake.'

The temperature in the room seemed to drop by ten degrees and Sara shivered.

'I've heard everything now,' Jake remarked coldly, swinging himself off the bed. 'You, of all people, saying you're concerned about my brother. That must be the biggest joke of the century.'

'He was my brother, too,' she said hotly.

'Stepbrother,' Jake corrected her brutally. 'And much good it did my father—or any of the rest of us—when you and your mother came to stay.'

'Leave my mother out of this,' snapped Sara.

'Willingly,' replied Jake. 'Since she seemed only too anxious to leave herself out of our family when she ran off to New York with that penniless painter.'

'She—' Sara stopped and bit her lip. She had promised herself a long time ago that she would not make excuses for her mother.

'She what?' inquired Jake. 'Come on, Sara, what psychobabble are you going to come up with to cover your mother's conduct?'

'What my mother did was her affair,' she replied as steadily as she could.

'She took my father for all the money she could get and then left us all in the lurch, including you, her own daughter.' The bitterness in Jake's voice took Sara aback.

'I'd no idea you cared so much,' she whispered.

'I'd no idea you cared so little,' Jake snapped back contemptuously. 'You obviously don't give a damn about your own flesh and blood, so lying about what happened to Jamie is probably no big deal as far as you're concerned.'

Sara's jaw dropped. 'That's not true,' she forced out. 'You've got it all wrong. You're just twisting the facts to suit yourself.'

'You're the one who's been twisting the facts,' corrected Jake.

'I've done nothing to be ashamed of!' Sara burst out.

But Jake swept on inexorably. 'So you keep saying. But you had Jamie on a string and you played him like a prize salmon.

'He was weak and charming and easily led—and boy, did you lead him. Everyone knows how he adored you. You could have been such a positive force in his life. But like mother, like daughter—all you did was spend his money,' he added grimly.

'And then one night, it seems, you had a furious row and shortly after that he got into his car and drove off a bridge. I don't call that nothing to be ashamed of.'

Sara pulled her hands from the table and wrapped her arms around herself, desperately needing protection, no matter how illusory, against his attack.

'It wasn't like that,' she said at last in a small voice, closing her eyes to shut out his gaze, but seeing instead pictures, horrible memories, racing through her mind.

'What was it like, then?' he said softly. 'Tell me.'

She hugged herself more tightly and gave a tiny shake of her head. 'I can't,' she whispered.

She knew without opening her eyes that he was standing close to her, but the touch of his cool hand on her hot face was so shocking, her whole body shuddered.

He slid his fingers around her neck and then down her spine, pulling her close to him.

'Open your eyes, Sara,' he said quietly, and she obeyed, looking at last up into his soft black gaze. 'What can you possibly be hiding that is so important?' he probed. 'What did you and Jamie say to each other that night?'

'Nothing, I tell you,' Sara replied desperately. 'It was just a . . . a silly row, that's all.'

A muscle thudded in Jake's cheek. 'Well, the inquest might have bought that, but I certainly don't. Especially when you won't say what the row was about.'

'It was just one of those ridiculous family tiffs,' snapped Sara. 'But how would you know?' she rattled on recklessly. 'You never stayed around long enough to really be part of the family.'

She could hear the blood rushing in her ears, and twisted her hands tightly together. Why was she goading him like this when all she wanted to do was run away and hide? Preferably in a nuclear bunker at least five thousand miles away.

She shot a look at his face and glanced hurriedly away. Talk about lighting the blue touch paper. Except that she was not standing well back from the fireworks that were sure to come.

'The verdict was misadventure, not suicide or unlawful killing, Jake,' she forced out. 'You can't blame me for his death. We may have had a . . . a misunderstanding, but I don't know why he skidded off the road. It's that simple.'

'So simple,' Jake repeated quietly, too quietly. 'Just a tiny little misunderstanding,' he added, his voice hardening. 'Well, that's all right, then, isn't it? All nice and neat, and you're in the clear.'

Sara swallowed. 'You must have grown very cruel indeed,' she whispered, 'if you think that his death doesn't affect me, that I don't wish every day that I could have stopped him from driving home that night. Whatever you say, he was my brother, too.'

' "Was" being the operative word,' Jake said searingly. 'Don't think, after that night, that you can claim a relationship with any of my family ever again.'

'Jake, I—' Sara choked out.

'Save it,' snapped Jake. 'I'm not interested in an apology you obviously don't mean. If everything is so open and above-board,' he pressed on, 'why won't you say what the row was about?'

Sara licked dry lips. 'I told you, I can't remember,' she said at last. 'In any case, it was between me and Jamie, and no one else.'

'And now you're just too ashamed of what happened that night to say any more about it,' Jake continued relentlessly. 'Don't you think Pa and I have a right to know, too?'

'No!' Sara burst out.

Anywhere on earth would be better than standing in this dusty room with Jake staring down at her as though he wished her in hell. She wanted to tell him about that night. Oh, how she wanted to. But Jamie's death had sealed her lips forever. And now she had not just lost a stepbrother, but her whole adoptive family.

There was silence in the room now and Sara raised her eyes to see Jake gazing thoughtfully at her. Almost as if he were thinking of a new method of attack.

His question when it came was totally unexpected. 'Are you trying to protect Jamie?'

'P-protect him?' she stuttered, her heart thudding. She had forgotten quite how shrewd Jake was. 'Why should I want to protect Jamie?'

He shrugged. 'I may have been away a lot, but I'm not totally blind. Jamie was very far from a perfect human being. He charmed people by saying the things he knew they wanted to hear—and then went his own sweet way.

'He charmed me—and I knew him better than anyone. He was lazy, selfish, but generally good-natured and willing to please—so long as it didn't cost him too much effort.

'He liked you—even loved you, I think, because you were all get up and go and afire with enthusiasm, and he could make believe that when he was in your company he was like that, too.'

'Stop it,' whispered Sara. 'I don't want to hear any more.'

'Why not?' replied Jake. 'Are you afraid of what else I may have figured out about you?'

'I don't care what you've figured out!' she yelled. 'You haven't seen me for years and yet just because your brother dies in a horrible accident an hour after he's seen me, you think you have some sort of God-given right to hound me to the ends of the earth.'

'Damn right, I have,' snarled Jake. 'Think about it, Sara. If you had been clever enough at the time of the crash to say, ''Oh, I'm sorry, Officer, but Jamie and I had a row over the fact that he's such a lousy driver, and he always goes too fast over that bridge,'' no one would have thought anything of it.

'In fact, you didn't even need to say you'd had a row. Why should you? Jamie was a lousy driver.

'But no. For some reason, known only to yourself, you have to reveal that the two of you had a row—and then, bang, you refuse to say what it's about. It's obvious you blurted out the truth and then decided you couldn't tell the whole story. I know you're hiding something, Sara. So why don't you save us all a lot more heartache and tell me what happened that night?'

'I can't,' she said pleadingly. 'I just can't. Please don't ask me any more, Jake. I don't care how badly you think of me, but Jamie meant a lot to me. And I can't say any more. It would only mean more hurt all round and I just...'

She swallowed desperately and blinked back the tears. Of all the moments to start crying, this had to qualify for the worst. She couldn't bear the thought of breaking down in front of him. And at best he would think she was merely trying to win some sympathy.

But when he spoke, he sounded weary, not furious. 'You always did seem to feel the need to stick up for him, didn't you, Sara? Even when you were children.'

'Well,' she said stiffly, 'I'm not a child any more, Jake.'

'No,' he whispered, pulling her close, his lips coming down on hers. 'I can quite see that.'

This could not be happening. Only a few seconds ago, he had practically accused her of being responsible for his brother's death. Now his mouth was claiming hers as though she were the only woman in the world.

For one haunting, delicious moment, she relaxed in his arms. She felt so safe, so right, and then she remembered another night, another world it seemed now, when they had kissed like this, and her heart flopped at the memory of the anguish that had followed.

A bitter lump rising in her throat, she pulled away. 'Stop it,' she said in a fierce, low voice. 'What are you trying to do to me—get by stealth what you can't get by threats?'

He looked down at her, his expression hardening. She shook herself like an angry cat and raised her hands to her heated face.

'That's what it was, wasn't it?' she accused. 'Just use any means in your power to get what you want out of me, and then walk away—' She stopped, pride refusing to let her add, Just like you did on that day so long ago.

He stared at her keenly, something in his eyes seeming to die. 'It appears you have almost as low an opinion of me as I have of you,' he said at last.

'Lower,' she muttered.

'I doubt it,' he replied grimly. 'But we've still got a job to do, however we feel about each other.'

She sighed. 'Is that what you said to Emma when you decided to bring me out here?'

A muscle thudded in his cheek. 'Leave her out of this,' he grated.

'I expect she'd love to hear you say that,' snarled Sara. 'What a pity I haven't got my tape recorder going. And if we'd set up your camera properly we could have had some wonderful holiday snaps to send to her.' They glared at each other, and to her astonishment Sara suddenly felt her heart sinking. 'Tell me,' she asked dully. 'Does Emma know about this honeymoon we're supposed to be on?'

Jake tipped up her chin to face him. 'I do believe you're jealous of her,' he said softly.

'Don't be ridiculous,' she spat. 'Jealous? Of what? Because of the silly way she talks about her "relationship" with you? And the stupid look she gives you when she wants your undivided attention and you're too busy doing something else?'

His lips curved slightly. 'Of course you're jealous, Sara. It's all very well mocking Emma, but the truth is you'd love to have some sort of steady "relationship" yourself. You just don't know how. You enter every affair you have with the sole idea of what you're going to get out of it at the end.'

Sara's jaw dropped. 'Every affair?' she repeated weakly. 'But I haven't—' She stopped abruptly and bit her lip.

Why on earth he should believe she was some sort of scarlet woman was completely beyond her. It was so untrue—so absolutely unfair. But then, what did she care what he thought?

'I don't give a toss what you think,' she said at last. 'Right at this moment, the whole country could blow up and I wouldn't care. And I'm so thirsty I'd accept a glass of water even from you.'

He motioned to the Thermos flask on the table. 'Help yourself,' he said coldly.

CHAPTER FOUR

JAKE watched expressionlessly as Sara took out a paper hanky from her handbag and carefully wiped one of the glasses on the table. It was quite clean, but any number of germs could be hiding in its many cracks.

Her hand shook as she poured the water into it and then raised it to her lips. 'I don't believe I'm here, you know,' she said defiantly. 'I'm just having a nightmare, and in a minute or two I'll wake up in my own bedroom and you and everything else here will be gone.'

He took the glass from her hand. 'In a few days, this will all be over for you,' said Jake. 'You'll go home and pick up your comfortable life—and all those rich boy-friends of yours.'

'Now just wait a minute,' Sara began hotly.

But he ignored her. 'This will just be something you can dine out on in all those expensive restaurants that you love to visit—providing, of course,' he added sardonically, 'that someone else is paying.'

She looked around for something to throw at him and her eye fell on the Thermos flask.

'I wouldn't bother,' said Jake, following her eyes and reading her intention as plainly as if she had spoken. 'I'd only throw it right back.'

'It isn't big enough to do you any lasting damage,' Sara said bitterly. 'What I need is a Thermos-nuclear missile.'

Jake reached out and tipped up her chin. 'Then we ought to go and collect your rucksack,' he drawled. 'The contents of that should give you plenty of ammunition.'

She wrenched herself away and glared furiously at him. 'What a brilliant idea,' she snapped. 'Now I'm only sorry I didn't manage to bring a cabin trunk. I'd have enjoyed heaving that at you.'

It was early evening but there were not many people on the streets and those that were kept staring at Sara.

'What's the matter?' she asked Jake in a low voice, moving instinctively closer to him.

He shrugged. 'Nothing much, except that I shouldn't think any of them have ever seen anyone in a short skirt before. Certainly not in the flesh anyway.'

Sara looked at one old man standing on a street corner, his face seemed and criss-crossed with a thousand wrinkles. She smiled uncertainly at him and he beamed widely back. 'Well, they seem friendly enough,' she said, staring doubtfully at the enormous knife stuck through the man's belt.

'They are,' Jake said firmly. 'It's mostly anyone from the army or government whom you have to watch. They're the ones in power and they're determined to hang on to it by any means they can. The ordinary man in the street is generally okay. Except that now he wants a share of that power and wealth, which is the short road to outright rebellion.'

They had reached the depot now. A truck in the centre of the yard was piled high with boxes and bales. 'That's our staff over there,' Sara said, pointing at their rucksacks.

Jake nodded. 'Stay here,' he ordered. 'I'll get them.'

He had not gone two paces when she felt a plucking at her skirt, and turning swiftly she found a soldier dressed in a baggy, ill-fitting green uniform grinning unpleasantly at her.

Fear at his expression flooded through her, and furious that she should feel so intimidated, she opened her mouth to tell him exactly what she thought of him.

Even though it was obvious he didn't understand English, no one could mistake her meaning. But before she had got more than a few words out, she was violently shoved from behind and half turned to see another soldier close beside her.

Within seconds, it seemed, she was surrounded by a small crowd of jostling, jeering soldiers. More terrified than she had ever been in her life, she tried to hit out with her handbag and opened her mouth to scream when she heard other, louder shouts.

The soldiers heard them, too, and as they turned from her, she felt a hand grip her wrist and begin pulling her away.

'Let go, you beast!' she yelled. 'Or so help me I'll kick you right where it hurts.'

'I'd like to see you try,' Jake said grimly in her ear. 'Now, will you stop yelling and get a move on?'

The little crowd of soldiers seemed to have evaporated. She looked at her wrist and the fingers that enclosed it and then up into his face. 'I thought you were someone else,' she said shakily. 'I—oh, Jake.' She swallowed the sob that was rising in her throat and shook her head. 'I'm sorry,' she muttered, trying to sound matter-of-fact, but longing to have the comfort of his arms around her and knowing it was the last thing she could ask for.

He began to hurry her away, but as her steps faltered, he stopped and briefly turned to look at her. Taken unawares, she cannoned against him, the feel of his hard body at once unsettling and completely familiar.

His eyes softened as he took in her white, stricken face and she gasped as his arm slid round her shoulders.

'It's all right,' he soothed in a voice that she hadn't heard for years. 'No one's going to hurt you.'

The cool cotton of his shirt was delicious against her tear-streaked face. 'I'm sorry,' she forced out. 'I know you don't like me, Jake, but—'

'It's all right,' he repeated, his kindness overwhelming her in a way the attack could never have done. 'You're safe now.'

She swallowed and pulled away with an effort. 'What happened to the soldiers?' she said in a low voice.

'They were called away on urgent business,' said Jake, picking up their bags and helping Sara on with her rucksack. 'In case you hadn't noticed it,' he added matter-of-factly, 'the depot's on fire.'

They slipped down a side street, hugging the walls against a flood of people who, it seemed, had materialized from nowhere and were all hurrying to see the blaze.

'Big day for them,' observed Jake. 'But someone will be made to pay for it, you can bet on it.'

'But it was an accident,' protested Sara.

Jake glanced sideways at her. 'Who says?' he inquired.

Her jaw dropped. 'Jake, you didn't—'

He shook his head. 'No, I most certainly did not. I was just about to plunge in among those soldiers around you when I saw two men running away fast, and then the building begin to go up. It seems like you probably have to thank the Bandhul rebels for your rescue.'

She stared at him, stung by the careful lightness of his tone after what she had just gone through. 'So no doubt, if it had been up to you,' she accused, 'you'd have just left me to the tender mercies of those appalling men?'

He gazed at her grimly and then pulled her into a doorway. 'Would you like me to take you back to the depot?' he grated. 'I could just leave you there, and good riddance.'

'You—you don't mean that,' she faltered.

There was silence and then he sighed heavily. 'No, I don't,' he said at last.

'It would solve all your problems,' Sara forced out. 'You wouldn't have to look at me any more and hate me because of Jamie.'

'Do you know how much I want to shake you sometimes?' he rasped.

'Yes,' she muttered.

She focused on a long smear of mud on his sleeve and then made herself look up into his eyes. To her astonishment, the lines in his face had relaxed and there was a faint smile on his lips. With an effort, she stopped herself from reaching out and touching his cheek. Why did he have to be so attractive?

'I never realized how much of a lethal weapon handbags were until I saw you in action with yours back there,' he murmured.

Sara swallowed. 'Why did you bother coming to my rescue, then?' she forced out.

His lips twisted. 'Someone had to protect those poor defenceless soldiers.'

'Big of you,' she whispered, noticing for the first time a large spreading bruise on his cheek-bone. There was blood on his knuckles, too, and wordlessly she rummaged in her handbag and handed him a paper hanky. 'Looks like they didn't much want to be protected,' she remarked, wiping his hand.

'They did put up some resistance,' he agreed and then looked at her straight. 'Tell me,' he inquired. 'Do you keep anything else in your handbag except tissues?'

'This bag is my self-preservation kit,' Sara said seriously. 'As you'd find out if you had one.'

His lips twitched. 'I'll pass on that, I think,' he said. 'Maybe I'll just rent out space in yours.'

'It's extremely practical,' she insisted.

'Like your skirt and those ridiculous shoes,' he mocked.

She pressed her lips together and said nothing. Their moment of closeness seemed to be over, like a mere trick of the light. And in any case, there was nothing to say in defence of her choice of clothes, because he had been proved absolutely right.

Jake crouched down over her rucksack and undid the straps, taking out the practical trousers, the boots and the sludge green socks. 'Here,' he said, handing them to her. 'Get them on now.'

'But it's the middle of the street,' she protested. 'And everybody's watching.'

'Two small children and a goat don't make up everybody, even in this town,' replied Jake. 'You're lucky the fire's such a big attraction, otherwise there'd be a cast of thousands to watch you put your trousers on.

'Now hurry up, before they all realize they might be much safer if they weren't anywhere near the depot.'

She glared at him and pulled the trousers up under her skirt. Then, unbuttoning the skirt, she eased it to the ground, stepped out of it and put on the socks and boots.

'Very chaste,' remarked Jake. 'You'll be quite safe now, going back to the hotel.'

'What do you mean?' she demanded. 'Where are you going?'

He looked at her in amazement. 'I'm a photographer, remember? So I'm going to get pictures of that fire.'

A cold hand clutched her heart. 'Jake, you can't,' she breathed. 'It's absolute madness. If the government's as rotten as you say, they're not going to take kindly to your taking pictures of civil unrest.'

'I've got a job to do,' he said stubbornly. 'And I'm going to do it.' He smiled grimly. 'You needn't worry. I'm not exactly going to ask any passing soldiers to smile and say cheese.'

Sara put her arms through the straps of her rucksack and heaved it onto her back. 'I'm coming with you,' she said.

'No,' he replied flatly. 'You're not cut out for this.'

'Well, it's a bit late to say that now,' she said bitterly. 'I'm a journalist and this is the job I've been sent on, remember? If you think I'm going meekly back to the hotel while there's a story happening right round the corner, then you are a couple of tacos short of the full combination platter.'

He stared at her impatiently. 'Sara, listen—'

'No,' she said, 'I'm not going to. You never listen to me. Why should I pay any attention to you? We'll either go together, or I'll make my own way there. Now which is it to be?'

He sighed and shrugged helplessly. 'Come on, then.' Bending down, he picked up her handbag. 'You better not forget this. It's probably got a couple of distress flares and a lifeboat in it.'

The crowds were milling ten deep around the depot, and apart from a few curious glances, no one paid the least attention to Sara and Jake. They were all too absorbed by the sight of the flames now licking through the wooden roof of the depot office. Soldiers had got a hose from somewhere and were training it on the building, but their efforts were hopeless.

'Stand real still,' whispered Jake, putting his hand on her shoulder and running off several shots with a tiny camera he was holding in the palm of his hand. 'I hope I'm going to get something after all this. I can't even take a light reading without announcing to the entire world what I'm doing.'

'I'm sure the people around us know exactly what we're up to,' replied Sara as she smiled uneasily at a woman gazing curiously at them.

Jake slid his camera into his pocket, put his arm around Sara and led her away. 'Time to go, I think,' he said. 'The Seventh Cavalry seemed to have arrived.'

They pressed back into the shadow of a wall as a string of trucks pulled up and disgorged more soldiers, who began barging among the crowds and pushing them away.

'Just walk slowly and look at me,' Jake said quietly, walking on again. 'We're on honeymoon, remember? The whole world could collapse and we just wouldn't notice.'

The hotel was in sight now and Sara quickened her pace. For all its admittedly basic charm, it now seemed to represent the last shreds of sanity and security in a world that was going completely mad.

She turned to speak to Jake and realized with a bolt of pure horror that he was no longer there. He must have gone back, she thought with a sickening thud. He had taken her in sight of safety and then left her to go and take some more of his ridiculous pictures.

Her jaw clenched and her heart raced as she thought of the soldiers he would be up against. She simply couldn't leave him to face that danger alone.

Sara stumbled back the way they had come, desperately hoping she would see Jake just a few yards ahead. But it was not until she was almost at the depot that she saw him, crouched in the shadow of a building, reeling off shot after shot of the blaze and the chaos it was creating.

What he couldn't see, because of the angle of the buildings, was a soldier aiming a gun at him from across the street. Sara's hand rose to her mouth in horror.

'Jake!' she yelled. 'Look out!'

Without even being truly conscious of what she was doing, she began to run towards him, screaming at him to move. But as she ran into the street, the soldier turned his aim to her and something sharp hit her in the arm and she fell to the ground with a cry.

She regained consciousness a few seconds later with the distinct impression that someone had dropped a rock on her, and then realized with almost light-headed relief that the weight on her back was merely her rucksack.

Her arm was throbbing painfully, and she probed it with shaking fingers, terrified of what she might find. Amazingly there was no sign of a bullet wound and she laid her head down again, weak with relief and astonishment.

It took a few more seconds for her to pluck up courage and look around. The fear that someone was just waiting to attack her as soon as she moved was literally paralyzing.

With an effort of will, greater than she had ever made, she forced herself to raise her head fully and saw in the light of the depot flames that what had promised to be a full-scale riot had been turned into knots of ragged resistance.

Soldiers were rounding up struggling men and soon, no doubt, they would be coming for her. But no one seemed to be looking in her direction. She raised herself to a crouching position, tears pouring down her face at the mental effort it cost, and looked back the way she had come.

In the shadows of the dark street, Sara could see a darker shadow moving and she froze, more terrified than she could ever remember being. Not even Jamie had scared her this much. The memory of that last night with him seemed almost ridiculous in comparison to this.

The shadow was moving again, and she knew it was coming towards her. Please, God, let it not be a soldier. And then guns cracked out in its direction and she bit back a scream as Jake scrambled to her side.

'What the hell do you think you're playing at?' he demanded in a hoarse whisper, adding before she could answer, 'Are you all right? Can you walk?'

'What I'm playing at?' she retorted, more relieved to see him than she would have thought possible even an hour ago. 'You nearly just got yourself killed slinking across the street like that.'

'At least I remembered to look both ways,' he said grimly, running his hands down her arms and legs and feeling the back of her head. 'Have you been hit anywhere?'

With a groan, she struggled to sit up. 'My arm hurts, but I don't think I've been shot. I don't really know what's happened to it,' she muttered. 'I'm sorry, Jake. I know it's only a matter of time now before we get picked up. We're in deep trouble and it's all my fault.'

'Remind me to ask you to repeat that tomorrow morning,' he said, looking around carefully before turning back to her. The expression on his face was not encouraging. 'Why did you come back?' he demanded. 'I took you right to the hotel.'

She stared at him and thought how close she had come to seeing him killed. 'I lost my handbag,' she forced out defiantly. 'What else?'

'You saved my life,' he said, shaking his head. 'You put yourself in danger to save me and damn near got yourself killed in the process. Why?'

The astonishment in his eyes was almost comical, she thought bitterly. Had he really thought so badly of her? She swallowed and looked him straight in the eye. 'It's just the sort of silly, shallow person I am, I suppose,' she said matter-of-factly. 'I'll try not to let it happen again.'

He said nothing, just stared grimly at her as she ploughed desperately on.

'Of course I came back. What do you think I am, Jake, unwanted luggage? Just to be left until called for?' She lifted her chin. 'And as you keep telling me, we're here to do a job. Both of us.'

'I don't believe I'm hearing this,' Jake bit out. 'It's almost too dark to be sure of getting decent pictures,' he grated. 'And it's certainly too dangerous to stand around and take notes. What were you planning on? Asking some rebel, on the off chance that he speaks English, for an exclusive interview?'

She shook off his arm and glared at him. 'Maybe,' she snapped. 'Why not? And if the light's so useless for photographs, what do you think you're playing at?'

He scowled down at her. 'I didn't say it was useless. I said it was uncertain. And I had a better than even chance of getting something.

'But you!' He stopped and breathed deeply. 'I never thought I'd see the day when I was in your debt, Sara. And I'm not sure I like it.'

She clutched her arm. 'You came back for me,' she said tiredly. 'We could call it quits if you like.'

He stared at her silently as gunfire cracked in the distance, and then, as if he had made up his mind about something, Jake grabbed her good arm and pulled her up. 'Come on,' he said grimly. 'Let's go.'

'Where?' she demanded, almost light-headed with pain and the relief of just being alive. And the feel of Jake's body against hers was more comforting than she would ever admit to anyone, even herself. 'Where are we going?'

His fingers cupped her face briefly. 'If we take it slowly, we might just make it back to the hotel. Want to try?'

She nodded with an effort.

'I know your rucksack's heavy,' he said gently. 'But you might be better keeping it on. It could help protect you from a stray shot.'

Sara glanced up at him with something like her old spirit and then grasped his arm. 'Anything you can do,' she began unthinkingly.

'I can do worse,' he said, completing their old childhood slogan and actually smiling at her. She was so amazed she tripped and he put out a hand to steady her. 'Come on, then,' he encouraged. 'Let's go while we can. The soldiers seem to have gone off up the other end of the street for the moment.'

As she stumbled against him, they made their way back in the shadows of the buildings. The streets were only fitfully lit, and the few people who passed them averted their eyes and hurried by.

The doors of the hotel were firmly barred, but after some determined knocking and shouting from Jake, the landlady opened up. Her face registered no surprise at all at their state, and it took only seconds before she had ushered them inside and secured the door behind them.

'Safe at last,' Sara muttered shakily, wanting to hug the woman. If only one of her arms didn't hurt quite so much.

Wearily she clumped after Jake up the stairs to their room, envying him his seemingly inexhaustible energy. If it hadn't been for him, she found herself thinking, she would still be lying terrified in that street, waiting for the soldiers to come and pick her up.

She laid a hand on his arm as he stopped at their door. But as their eyes met, she bit her lip. This was going to be more difficult than she had thought. 'Don't tell me,' said Jake, his mocking tones belying the gentle look in his eyes. 'You've suddenly realized you've dropped your make-up bag by the depot and can we go back for it.'

'Actually,' she bit out, 'I wanted to say thank-you for...' She swallowed hard and then added firmly, 'For saving my life back there. I behaved very stupidly and I'm sorry.'

He looked at her for a long moment and then, tipping her chin up, kissed her full on the lips.

Stunned, she stared at him as he drew back and smiled wickedly at her. 'What was that for?' she muttered in amazement.

He shrugged. 'Rejoining the human race, I guess. And if you've got the guts to apologize, so have I.'

Speechless, she watched him throw open the door and then followed him in, suddenly more tired than she could ever remember feeling before.

Jake shrugged off his rucksack and dropped it on the floor.

The thud seemed to split her head in two, and all of a sudden the room was twirling very slowly around her. 'I can't seem to get my rucksack off,' murmured Sara, her body crumpling as she fell in a dead faint in his arms.

It was broad daylight when she awoke in bed, her arms around Jake's neck, her head pillowed on his shoulder. She sat up with a start and then realized with a bolt of horror that she had no clothes on.

Their sleeping bags had been zipped together—obviously by Jake. But what else had he done? She pulled a pillow towards her and hugged it, staring warily at him. What had happened last night?

He slept so easily, his ridiculously long eyelashes coal black against his tanned face. Almost without realizing it, she lifted a finger to gently trace the outline of his bruised cheek-bone, and then gasped in shock as his own hand circled her wrist.

'There's no point in trying to poke me in the eye, Sara,' he said lazily and in a voice that was all too awake. 'It won't get you home any sooner.'

His eyes were open now, regarding her with an amused tolerance that made her grit her teeth. 'I wasn't—' she began, and then stopped dead. How could she tell him that he was awakening feelings in her that were best left firmly asleep?

'Wasn't what?' he prompted.

Sara opened her mouth to tell him exactly where to get off, and then gazed at him accusingly, trying hard to calm the furious thudding of her heart. 'Why haven't I got any clothes on?' she blurted out at last.

He gazed back at her blandly. 'Why do you think?'

She pulled the pillow more tightly to herself and backed away as far as she could from him. 'How could you take advantage of me like that?' she gasped. 'Just because I let you kiss me. How could you?'

He leaned out of bed and passed her a T-shirt from the top of his rucksack. 'Here,' he offered.

'You might have the decency to get me some of my clothes,' she said tightly.

'I'm not a decent sort of person,' he drawled. 'Besides, I'm extremely comfortable where I am.'

'Close your eyes, then,' she ordered.

'Bit late for that, wouldn't you say?' he said silkily.

'What do you mean?' she gasped, disturbing pictures forming in her mind. 'We haven't...you didn't? I mean, you wouldn't. Did—did we...?'

A slow smile spread across his face. 'Make love, you mean?' he inquired.

She nodded speechlessly, her face beginning to burn scarlet.

He touched her cheek briefly and raised an eyebrow. 'Well, well, Sara Thornton blushing. I never thought I'd see the day.'

'You're the one who ought to be going red with shame,' she spat. 'How dare you behave like that?' A little muscle was pounding in his cheek and she longed to slap him right on it, but she couldn't move her hands without the risk of dropping the pillow and utterly exposing herself. 'You are the pits, Jake,' she said furiously, angry tears threatening to spill down her face.

'Was that an assessment of my character, or sexual prowess?' he asked.

'Both!' she replied wildly, gasping as his hand grasped her shoulder and forced her back down on the bed. He leaned over her, his eyes gazing deep into hers.

'You know, it's a strange thing,' he said. 'But I don't remember anything about this so-called lovemaking last night, either. Why don't we just take the opportunity now to refresh our memories?'

His nearness on the plane had been disturbing enough. Now as he half lay across her, she felt as though all the air had suddenly been knocked out of her lungs. Every sense in her was alive to him—the faint smell of his lemon aftershave, the silky satin feel of his inner arm as it rested against her body. All she was conscious of seeing were his eyes, soft as pools of ink.

She licked dry lips and remembered with a pang the taste of his kiss the evening before.

'Well, Sara?' he demanded softly. 'What conclusion have you come to? Did we make love last night? Or not?' His voice was low, husky, and her blood was thundering in her ears. 'I must admit,' he added silkily, 'it's not very flattering to my ego that you can't remember anything at all.'

'You don't sound very crushed,' Sara forced out, tearing her eyes away from his and willing herself to focus on his left ear. She couldn't possibly be affected by that, she told herself as firmly as she could.

'This ability of yours to forget things seems terribly inconvenient. For you as well as everyone around you,' he continued smoothly. 'But you wouldn't believe the strides medical science has apparently made in this field. You could get treatment for it.'

He paused. 'On the other hand, perhaps you just don't want to remember things that make you feel uncomfortable and guilty, hmm?'

'Jake, I—' she began, but his lips stopped hers, his hand cupping the full softness of her breast.

'Remember anything yet?' he whispered, his lips dropping to her throat, moving caressingly over her warm flesh.

It was unthinkable that something like this could have happened between them last night, leaving no memory whatsoever.

'What about Emma?' she forced out at last, willing herself not to slide under his spell. 'So much for her "understanding" with you, if you can behave like this, Mr Holier-Than-Thou Armstrong.'

'Emma?' he said, startled.

'Yes, Emma,' snapped Sara, taking the opportunity to wriggle away and pull the sleeping bag up to her chin. 'Remember her? Blonde, ambitious, wears a bit too much eye make-up. You know, the one you have the "understanding" with.'

'The only person Emma has an understanding with is herself,' Jake replied searingly.

'You're such a liar,' Sara gasped after a shocked silence. 'And that's the nicest thing I can say about you. Last night I fainted at your feet, and all you do is take my clothes off and...' She paused and began to flame scarlet again.

'And what?' he said quietly, mockingly. 'What did I do?'

His eyes, as soft as Tarmac, rose to meet hers, and she gasped in surprise at the message in them. 'You didn't do anything!' she exclaimed.

He drew back and nodded slowly. With a cry, she scrambled as far from him as she could. 'What's the matter?' he said sardonically. 'Disappointed?'

'Disappointed!' she spat, her body trembling uncontrollably. 'I'd rather have made love to one of those soldiers at the depot last night.'

'I don't think love figured too highly in their plans for you,' remarked Jake. 'Otherwise they'd have handed you a bunch of flowers before they attacked you.'

'That's pretty cynical even coming from you,' she retorted.

He bowed his head briefly in mock penitence. 'Sorry, ma'am. I forgot I was talking to a sensitive, romantic soul who thinks stars are God's daisy chain.'

Sara glared at him. 'At least those soldiers were honest about what they wanted,' she flung back. 'How dare you pretend you've my best interests at heart and then treat me like this?'

His face hardened. 'That's where you're wrong, Sara,' he said coldly. 'I've never pretended that I had your best interests at heart. And that's something you better not forget again.'

She shivered involuntarily. It was as though the Jake she had known had reappeared only to lull her into a false sense of security. She gazed at him mutely, trying to find something in common between the boy who had dominated her childhood and the cruel stranger whose bed she now shared.

A lump rose in her throat and desperately she swallowed. 'Why are you like this, Jake?' she forced out. 'What happened to you?'

For a moment, his eyes softened and then he shook his head impatiently. 'I could ask the same question,' he remarked. 'What happened to you, Sara? To that eager, sparkling girl who could charm the world?'

'The world moved on,' Sara replied bitterly. 'And the girl got left behind.'

She looked away and hugged the sleeping bag more closely to her. Damn Jake and his stupid, probing questions. They were getting far too close for comfort and she didn't know if she could trust herself not to give everything away. What on earth was she doing here?

On impulse, she grabbed the T-shirt he had handed her and thrust it angrily over her head, getting it hopelessly tangled in the process. One of the armholes seemed to have completely disappeared, and her head was swathed in cotton.

It was so shaming she wanted to cry. She felt so exposed and she knew that Jake was watching her. 'Here,' he offered, 'let me help.'

'Don't touch me!' she screeched. 'I'm doing fine by myself.'

'Somehow I don't think so,' he said softly, his hands brushing tantalizingly against her skin. Two sharp tugs pulled the cotton away from her face. 'Lift your right arm,' he ordered. She glared into his eyes from six inches away and obeyed. 'Now.' He pushed her hand through the appropriate hole and pulled the cotton straight.

'How could you?' she accused, desperately trying to retain some of her dignity.

He shrugged, deliberately misunderstanding her. 'It was quite simple,' he said. 'I just took an edge of the cotton and tugged. It generally does the trick, although I must say I'm more accustomed to taking clothes off than helping someone put them on.'

'You know what I mean,' she grated. 'You led me to believe that I...that we made love last night.'

He shook his head gently. 'No, Sara, you led yourself to believe that. You should know that any woman I make love to is completely aware of everything that is going on.' He smiled straight into her flushed, angry face. 'And enjoying it, too,' he added softly.

'So why did you take all my clothes off?' she demanded heatedly.

He reached for a pillow and leaned back comfortably. 'Actually, I didn't,' he said. 'After you fainted last night, I must admit I stripped you down to your underwear to check exactly how badly you were hurt.

'That soldier who shot at you must have hit the wall behind and you were then hit by a piece of flying stone or something. Your arm's pretty badly bruised, and I'm no doctor, but I guess it'll be okay.'

Sara looked down at her aching left arm and remembered with sudden vividness how Jake had braved those gunshots to save her. 'Thank you,' she said stiffly.

He shrugged. 'All in a day's work.'

She gazed at him, her expression hardening. 'I suppose you're going to tell me I took the rest of my clothes off myself?'

He yawned and nodded, looking suddenly bored. 'You were freezing cold but kept muttering how hot you were, and I couldn't get any clothes on you, so I zipped our sleeping bags together and hoped our combined body heat would keep you warm. You must have taken the rest of your stuff off all by yourself in the middle of the night.'

'I don't believe you,' grated Sara.

Jake shrugged. 'I don't care.'

She glared at him and then, swearing horribly under her breath, rummaged down in the depths of the soft, downy bags. She emerged, a few seconds later, holding her underclothes. Why did he have to be so right all the time? 'I really hate you, Jake Armstrong,' she snarled.

'I doubt it,' he said, shrugging and, picking up a paperback book from the floor, began to read it as though it was the most interesting thing in the world.

'Where's the bathroom?' she demanded.

He looked at her over the top of the book. 'What bathroom?' he asked mildly.

'Oh, come on, Jake,' she protested. 'Don't be ridiculous. There's got to be a bathroom.'

'There is a rather primitive shower a few doors down,' he conceded at last.

'Thank you,' she snapped. 'That sounds fine. Anybody would think I was demanding sunken marble and gold taps.'

Jake's eyes glinted with humour. 'Sorry,' he said, not sounding at all apologetic. 'I forgot for a moment what a practical down-home kind of girl I'm dealing with.'

'If you call me vain once more,' Sara said through gritted teeth, 'I'll—'

Jake's eyebrows rose. 'Cut off all your hair and invest in sackcloth and ashes?' he supplied innocently.

She glared at him and, grabbing a towel and soap, fled for the shower, the sounds of his laughter ringing in her ears.

CHAPTER FIVE

JAKE had been right. The shower had been pretty basic, but the water was hot, and the feel of soap on her skin cheered Sara immeasurably.

She found herself smiling tentatively at Jake as she passed him on the way back to their room. And to her absolute surprise, he actually grinned back.

He was completely different when he smiled, she thought with a pang. The grim lines smoothed out, his lips full and generous. She looked at the towel he carried and said meaningfully, 'The shower was marvellous. I can't think why you felt I wouldn't like it.'

His lips twitched. 'No,' he agreed with deceptive mildness. 'In fact, you've been in there so long I thought you'd been washed away.'

'Sorry to disappoint you,' she said automatically, hating herself immediately for the childish bitterness of her tone.

Damn Jake and his easy sense of humour. Why did she have to feel so wrong-footed by him? she thought as she finished dressing in their room.

Tying her bootlaces with sudden savagery, she paid no attention to the door being noisily booted open. 'Oh, just barge in, why don't you, Jake?' she snapped sarcastically. 'And let the world and his wife watch me getting dressed.'

But the footstep that thudded across the floor were not Jake's, and as she slowly raised her head and then sat up, her blood ran cold at the sight of her visitors.

Three men dressed in army green were standing around her. Another in civilian clothes stood by the door. 'What do you want?' she gasped, trying hard to look calm and unfazed.

One of the soldiers, obviously an officer of some kind, spoke and the civilian translated. 'It is what you want that we would like to know,' he said in clipped, precise English.

'I don't understand,' Sara replied slowly, her heart pounding, and then, trying hard to keep the tremor out of her voice, demanded, 'What have you done with Jake?'

'Jake?' One of the men stepped towards her and Sara, remembering the previous night at the depot only too vividly, instinctively shrank away.

'My—' She swallowed and then went on more steadily, 'My husband. We're on our honeymoon. What have you done with him?'

'It's all right, darling, I'm right here.' Jake was standing in the doorway, and the men turned to face him. But he ignored them, calmly walking towards Sara and helping her to her feet. 'Are you all right?' he asked in an undertone, throwing his washing kit on the bed.

She nodded quickly, relief flooding through her at his closeness.

'Well, gentlemen,' he demanded, squeezing her hand and turning to the soldiers, 'what can we do for you?'

'What did you have to do with the fire at the depot yesterday?' One of the soldiers rested his hand on the gun at his belt and Sara's heart gave a double thud. Jake looked as though someone had merely asked him for directions to the nearest post office.

'We had nothing to do with it. We were collecting our luggage when the fire started,' he said. 'I have to say my wife was subjected to the most awful harassment by your men, and then when we tried to return to our hotel, someone shot at us.' He took a step towards the most senior-looking officer, and the man stepped back involuntarily. 'In fact,' Jake grated, 'I feel like complaining to your commanding officer about the whole affair. Perhaps you would be good enough to give me his name?'

The soldier swallowed and the civilian laid a hand on Jake's sleeve. 'There has obviously been a misunderstanding,' he said placatingly.

'Obviously,' Jake ground out.

The soldiers spoke among themselves and then left the room with the civilian, a dapper little man in sunglasses and an ill-fitting suit, following. He turned in the doorway and looked back searchingly at Jake and Sara. 'Honeymooners are welcome in Bandhul,' he said as matter-of-factly as if he were telling them a bus timetable. 'Spies are not.'

Sara watched them go and then sat limply on the bed. 'You all right?' Jake asked softly.

'Yes,' she said shakily. 'But what was that all about?'

'It was a warning,' he replied. 'And it means we haven't got much time left.' He strode to the table and poured some water into a glass and handed it to her. 'Here.' Her fingers were shaking so much she spilled some of the water down her shirt. Jake sat down next to her and put his arm round her. 'Nothing bad is going to happen to us, Sara.'

'I wish I could believe that,' she whispered.

'Hey,' he said smiling, tipping up her chin and gazing into her eyes, 'we're on our honeymoon, remember?'

Tears threatened to spill down her face at his light, bantering tone, but she blinked them away determinedly. 'They must think us pretty mad honeymooners, then, coming here when we could be sipping banana daiquiris in some Caribbean paradise, like normal people seem to do.'

'Quite mad,' he agreed. 'But we just wanted to be alone.'

Sara giggled in spite of herself. 'It doesn't matter what you do, Jake. You'll never sound like Greta Garbo.' His full lips curved and she stared at him, her heart thundering. 'That's the second time you've smiled in the past five minutes,' she said shakily. 'You want to be careful. It could become a habit.'

They went out to the market to buy their breakfast, pushing their way through sullen-seeming crowds to get to the food stalls. 'The people here don't seem half as cheerful as the ones we saw when we arrived last night,' observed Sara.

'Judging from that visit we had from those soldiers,' replied Jake, 'I should think there's been a pretty big crack-down since the depot fire. Can't you feel the tension in the air?'

Sara looked at him and then turned away hurriedly. The only tension she could feel was the one gluing up her whole body at Jake's presence. 'I—I hadn't really noticed,' she stammered at last.

He gave her a strange, searching look and then turned his attention back to the stalls. 'What about some walnuts?' he suggested.

'Walnuts?' she echoed uncomprehendingly.

He nodded. 'They certainly seem to be the dish of the day as far as this market is concerned. Of course, you could always have walnuts instead. Or even walnuts.' Sara bit her lip and looked at the ground, her mind miles away. Jake reached out and tipped up her chin to face him. 'Sara?'

The touch of his fingers made her heart do a double somersault. 'What?' she quavered.

'I'd never have brought you here if I thought you weren't going to smile even a little bit at my appalling jokes.'

His tone mocking, his eyes gentle, he held her gaze and she swallowed hard. The message was unspoken but unmistakable. This was the last place on earth to go to pieces. 'Guess we'll have to have walnuts, then,' she managed.

He nodded slowly and smiled. 'Attagirl,' he encouraged, and turning to the stallholder he began a skilful dumb show to bargain for their breakfast.

They walked back to the hotel slowly, Jake cradling the big bag of nuts, while Sara's arms were full of tinned mandarin oranges and a jar of fresh yoghurt, which she had spotted an old peasant woman selling. 'Nuts and yoghurt,' murmured Jake, almost to himself. 'I never thought you—'

'Don't say it.' Sara rounded furiously on him and he stopped, looking quizzically down at her.

'Don't say what?' he inquired.

'Don't say you never thought you'd see the day when I ate yoghurt and walnuts for breakfast,' she ground out. 'I've had just about as much as I can take from you about my so-called expensive tastes.'

One of his eyebrows ever so slightly rose and then he smiled at her. It was one of his most devastating weapons, she thought suddenly and was hard put not to smile back.

Instead, she scowled even more fiercely at him and continued hurriedly, 'Anyone would think I was born in the lap of luxury, the way you keep taking the mickey out of me. Well, I won't have it, Jake.'

He opened his mouth, but she swept on, unwilling to let him do anything to stop her sudden flow of assertiveness.

'You should know, more than most, that until my mother married your father and I came to stay in your house that I'd had a pretty hard childhood. Luxury was not something that I knew much about.'

'So what are you doing now,' Jake asked sardonically. 'Making up for lost time?'

She glared at him and clutched the jar of yoghurt more tightly. 'You are so bloody arrogant, do you know that?' she accused. 'If anyone takes luxury and people and the services they give for granted, I'd say it was you, Jake Armstrong.'

It was his turn to look utterly amazed now. 'Me?' he questioned.

'Yes, you,' she said, nodding vigorously. 'Anything you wanted to do when we were children, Jamie and I always had to fall in with. And when we grew up, nothing changed. You wanted to swan off and go round the world and then get into news photography, leaving Jamie to be a dutiful son—well, that's what happened.

'You wanted me to go to Bandhul, when I've never done this sort of reporting in my life—and everybody, including me, immediately clicks their heels.'

There was silence and she made herself meet Jake's eyes to find him gazing thoughtfully at her. 'I didn't notice there was much clicking of heels from your direction when I suggested you come out here,' he said drily.

'I didn't notice there was much of a suggestion in the way you ordered me around,' retorted Sara.

He looked at her more closely. 'Are you trying to blame me in some obscure way for Jamie's death?' he probed.

She bit her lip and then shook her head. 'No, I suppose not,' she said in a low voice. 'Only Jamie could have stopped himself from pushing the self-destruct button. But maybe all of us should shoulder some of the guilt for getting him to that point.'

Jake, his face darkening, grasped her shoulder and shook her a little. 'Are you saying my brother killed himself?' he rasped.

Sara stared at him, her eyes suddenly huge with unshed tears. 'I don't know what I'm saying,' she whispered. 'I thought it was so clear in my mind what had happened, and now I don't know what to think any more.' His grip tightened on her shoulder, but she shook it off and stood back. 'Just leave me alone, Jake,' she forced out. 'Leave me alone!' and with a sob she turned on her heel and ran back to the hotel.

Her heart hammering, Sara pounded up the wooden steps to the third floor, and then not wanting to re-enter their dismal little bedroom, she kept on going past the doorway and found herself standing on a flat rooftop.

There was a table by the parapet, and with a sigh she flopped down into one of the rickety chairs beside it and put her head in her hands. What had she done?

She heard steps behind her and lifted her tear-stained face quickly, like an animal that smells danger. It was Jake. His face expressionless, he put his packages on the table and sat down.

She stared at him, every sense on the alert.

'We have to talk,' he said grimly.

'Do we?' she replied recklessly.

He sighed impatiently. 'You can't hide the truth from me forever, Sara, and you're silly to try.'

'Well, I'll just have to be silly, then,' she said woodenly. 'It's what you expect of me after all, isn't it?'

His jaw clenching, he turned to prise a loose stone from the mouldering parapet and used it to crack open a walnut.

'Is that the technique you're going to use on me?' she forced out.

'I wasn't going to be quite so subtle,' he said grimly, leaning over the table to hand her some of the nuts. She took them with shaking fingers. 'You can start talking as soon as you're ready,' he said quietly, 'so long as it's in the next five minutes.'

She licked dry lips. 'I—' she began, and then stopped as she saw two figures approaching their room. 'Oh, no,' she whispered with a sinking heart. 'Not more soldiers.'

Jake stood up. 'They're monks,' he said, his hand shading his eyes against the blinding sunshine. 'At least, one's a monk. The other is just a boy.'

Sara half turned to look more closely at the pair's maroon robes and the infinitely kind, peaceful expression on the old monk's face. She wondered how she could ever have mistaken him for a soldier.

'What do you think they want?' she whispered.

Jake shrugged. 'Haven't the faintest. But they certainly don't mean any harm. They literally wouldn't hurt a fly.'

'They're going into our room!' breathed Sara.

She jumped up and would have run after them, but Jake put a restraining hand on her shoulder. 'Gently,' he murmured. 'Just take it easy.'

He gazed at her, holding her eyes until the immediate tension eased out of her body, and then dropped his hand and walked unconcernedly to their room. Sara, trembling from the unexpected contact, her mind seething with unspoken questions, followed.

They found the monk, leaning for support on the boy, standing in the middle of the room staring benignly at the clothes and possessions spilling out of their rucksacks.

'Can we help you?' Jake asked amiably. Sara glanced at him, suddenly remembering with blinding clarity just how charming he could be. Not that he would ever be like that to her again.

The boy, head shaven and not more than fifteen, looked solemnly at them and then asked very slowly, 'What are your names?'

Jake gave them, and the monk, listening to the boy, smiled.

'You are from the West?' the boy added. Jake nodded.

There was a small silence and then the monk spoke. The boy looked at Jake and then at Sara.

'His name is Lama Banideya,' he said at last. 'He wishes you good fortune.' They each clasped their hands together and bowed, and after a moment Jake and Sara did likewise, watching in silence as their two visitors left.

'What on earth was that all about?' she demanded as soon as she was sure they were out of earshot.

Jake shrugged. 'Who can say? Buddhist monks, especially in this part of the world, are a law unto themselves.'

They walked slowly back to the table outside, both busy with their own thoughts, and sat down to their breakfast once more.

Sara glanced at Jake several times as she ate, expecting him to go on the attack again about Jamie, but to her surprise he remained silent and obviously preoccupied.

Unwilling to do anything that might draw his fire again, she ate as quietly as she could, trying to figure out any number of ways in which she could fend off his questions when they eventually came, as they almost certainly would.

Despite her shower, her hair felt like coconut matting because of the fine dry dust that blew everywhere. But the sun was hot on her back and she flexed her shoulder-blades like a cat in front of a gas fire. The sunshine had to be the only good thing about this place.

She dug savagely into the yoghurt with her camping spoon and looked up at Jake. 'I know you expect this of me,' she said defiantly, unable to stay silent any longer. 'But I think we should get the hell out of here as soon as possible. We stick out like sore thumbs, and it seems everybody is watching us. This is not a healthy place to be, Jake, and I want to be able to collect my pension someday. Preferably while I'm still in one piece.'

Jake levered open the tin of oranges with his penknife and gazed at her thoughtfully. 'You're right,' he said. She could feel her whole body relax with relief, but before she could say anything, he continued, 'It was just the sort of thing I expected you to say.'

'Why, you—' she began angrily.

But he held up his hand. 'Look, Sara, it doesn't really matter what you think, or what I think, for that matter. The whole point is that we're stuck here until we can get the next plane out.

'Now, we can either sit in our room and you can tell me all about Jamie—which you will do in any case—'

'I will not,' she interrupted fiercely.

'Or we can attempt to do what we're paid for,' Jake continued relentlessly. 'There's nothing to stop our doing a bit of sightseeing and maybe picking up some information along the way.'

'And a couple of stray bullets, if we're very lucky,' Sara added grimly.

'Oranges?' he offered, pushing the tin towards her.

She sighed. 'I suppose you're right, as usual,' she agreed finally, spearing up some of the fruit and glaring at him. 'So long as we're careful.'

He cracked open some more walnuts in the following silence and smiled challengingly at her. 'Pity you couldn't have given yourself that piece of advice last night,' he said silkily.

She clenched her jaw. 'Sometimes even the most reasonable person can be goaded into doing something silly.'

'Yes,' he sighed theatrically. 'You're right, of course. I should never have bothered rescuing you.'

'That's not what I meant,' she forced out. 'And you know it.'

'Do I?' he said gently. 'Perhaps you should stop taking offence so easily, Sara, and start thinking about the job in hand. That way, we might both get out of here in one piece.'

She scraped out the last of her yoghurt in furious silence. How dare he patronize her like that? How dare he? Everything that had happened to her was all his fault. And she was never going to let him forget it. Not in one thousand years.

Sara sat back and stared into the middle distance. Nothing would have induced her at that moment to look at Jake. It was a few seconds before she realized that the sky above them was such a clear blue she could see the moon, pale and wraithlike, hovering over the distant mountain peaks.

Jake was right, of course, damn him. She took everything he said to her as a personal insult and it wasn't helping an already difficult situation. Trouble was, it was Jake who had put her in this spot in the first place.

'What's the matter?' he probed. 'You looked miles away.'

'I was just thinking,' she said frankly, 'that we seem to have spent all these years avoiding each other, and now we couldn't be closer if we tried.'

'Oh, we could get a lot closer than this, Sara,' Jake replied seriously. 'Trouble is, I'm not sure I want to get stung twice.'

Her face reddened and her gaze slid from his. 'You seem to have this completely false opinion of me,' she forced out. 'And I can't seem to do anything to change it.'

Jake opened his mouth to reply and then, alerted by a noise coming from their room, turned his head in astonishment.

Sara, following his gaze, saw two soldiers standing by the door. The civilian of their earlier encounter came out of their room and walked towards them.

'What the—' began Jake, standing up.

'Good morning,' said the man. 'A late breakfast I see, but not a particularly appetizing one.'

'We were just saying how lovely it was,' Sara replied stubbornly, refusing to meet Jake's eyes.

The man nodded slowly, the sunshine flashing off his glasses. 'I do not think ''lovely'' is perhaps the correct description. But it is not good for strangers such as yourselves to stay in a place like this.'

'What's wrong with it?' Sara demanded hotly.

He smiled at her. 'It does not cater very well for westerners. I know a much better place.'

Jake stared at him calmly. 'We're quite happy here, thanks. It's quiet, central, and we don't really mind about the amenities.'

The man shrugged and spread his hands. 'That is most kind. Unfortunately, the rooms in this hotel are all booked by other people from tonight onwards. And we in the Government Tourist Agency—' he waved vaguely as if to include the soldiers '—are concerned that you should have more appropriate accommodation.'

Fear caught at Sara's throat and wordlessly she reached for Jake's hand. 'Where did you have in mind?' Jake inquired offhandedly, returning the pressure of her fingers.

The man smiled broadly. 'We will take you to the hotel our western visitors normally use. The remainder of our guests there flew home earlier this week, but honeymooners need no extra company, so I am told.'

His beam, if anything, grew wider and Sara resisted the urge to throw the bag of walnuts at him.

'You will find it has all the amenities you are used to,' he continued. 'And we can arrange for you to visit one or two of our beautiful temples before you fly home at the end of the week.' He held out their passports. 'I have already taken the liberty of relieving you of these. So much more convenient all round. You can have them back when you leave.'

'But—' began Sara.

'Unfortunately, there are certain criminal elements in the city at the moment,' replied their visitor. 'It would be safer if you went home on the next plane.'

Jake, a muscle jerking in his cheek, squeezed Sara's hand so tightly she almost winced. Then, as if he had come to a decision, he shrugged. 'It seems we have no choice.'

The man from the Government Tourist Agency beamed again and shook his head. 'None whatsoever,' he agreed.

They repacked their rucksacks under the careful gaze of the soldiers and were escorted down to the front door, where a jeep was waiting.

Sara watched the door of the hotel close behind them and twisted round in her seat to keep it in view as long as possible while the Jeep headed out of the city.

'What's the matter?' Jake said quietly. 'Can't believe you're actually leaving the worst hotel in civilization?'

She glanced up at the grim lines in his face, and her hand lifted as she thought of touching his cheek. But what was the use? Her fingers dropped back into her lap. 'Actually,' she said as matter-of-factly as she could, 'I was thinking how safe I felt there.'

He gazed at her with a look she could not read, but before he could say anything, the Jeep, now a few miles out of town, turned into a long, curving drive, bordered with grass and flowers, and stopped before a low, white-washed building.

Their feet echoed on the clean tiles of the reception area, and their escort, after a short talk with the man behind the desk, handed them a key. 'It is for the honeymoon suite,' he said with a smile. 'Enjoy the rest of your stay,' and, bowing in the most amiable fashion, he turned and left.

Only the guns slung over the shoulders of the two soldiers outside by the Jeep gave any clue at all to the fact that Jake and Sara had been taken to this place against their will.

'Would you believe that?' breathed Sara, watching them go.

'Why not?' Jake shrugged. 'They've got us absolutely where they want us. We can't complain of maltreatment and we can't go nosing about talking to unsuitable people. Most important of all, we'll be sent back where we belong at the end of the week. Very neat.'

'But what is this place?' she asked as two boys shouldered their bags and the man from the reception desk came out to lead them up a couple of flights of stairs to their room.

'Like the man said, it's where those groups of western tourists come, I suppose,' replied Jake. 'They're kept in comfort, taken round to see all the temples and so forth without ever really being allowed a look at the true Bandhul.'

The door to their room was made of some beautifully carved dark wood and Sara gasped as the receptionist threw it open. A big, high, deep bed dominated the charmingly whitewashed room, which was floored in mosaic tiles. There was also a window looking out on the mountains, but it was closely barred.

A door led off the room and she couldn't help turning to Jake with her eyes sparkling as she saw what lay beyond it. 'An *en suite* bathroom!' Then worriedly she looked at the man. 'Does it work?'

He shrugged, obviously perplexed. 'Any time you want,' he said at last and, shaking his head at the madness of foreigners, wandered away down the corridor and left them to it.

Sara shrugged off all her clothes and switched on the shower. It had only been a few hours since her first one that morning, but already she felt so dusty again that the thought of clean water on her skin was irresistible.

Nothing happened, and she stared in frustration at the gleaming chrome rose. 'I might have known it,' she muttered, giving the pipes a vicious thwack. Two seconds later, she was hit in the face by a powerful jet of icy water and she screamed in shock.

The door banged open and the shower curtain was ripped away. 'What the hell's going on?' demanded Jake above the thunder of the water.

He reached to switch off the taps, and she glared at him, yanking the curtain back across her body. 'I would have thought it was perfectly obvious what was going on,' she snapped. 'I was having a shower.'

His eyes dropped from her hair, snaking wetly over her shoulders and on down her water-sleek body. 'The way you screamed,' he replied grimly, 'I thought you were entertaining an axe murderer. Or at the very least, those soldiers from the depot.'

'The water was cold, and it came out when I wasn't expecting it,' she said with some asperity.

His lips twitched. 'Of course,' he said, shrugging. 'How silly of me. I mean, I always take it for granted that when I switch a shower on I'm going to get a faceful of water, but you, being the intrepid journalist that you are, probably expect anything but.'

Sara swept the water out of her eyes. 'Do you know you're absolutely—'

But Jake carried on regardless. 'Tell me,' he said interestedly. 'What did you think was going to come out of the spray—champagne and chocolates? Must have been quite a shock to the system when you got a dose of plain old cold water in the face.'

Sara stamped her foot and to her horror found herself slipping on the tiles. But Jake shot out a hand and held her steady.

'What do you do when you have a shower at home, Sara?' he inquired, his gentle tones masking the corrosive sarcasm of his words. 'Since it's obviously one of your more dangerous assignments?'

She pushed her hair out of her face and glared at him. 'I invite round all those boyfriends you think I've got so they can hold me steady. What else?' she snapped.

He was pulling her closer to him now and there was nothing she could do about it. The shower curtain stuck clammily to her body and he looked at it as though he had never seen one before. 'Is this what the best-dressed women are wearing in the shower these days?' he murmured, his fingers sliding under the thin, clear plastic.

The breath caught in her throat. 'Jake, I—'

'Go on,' he said interestedly. 'Is this the point where you attempt to seduce me, hoping that I'll become so ensnared by your charms that I'll forget all about getting the truth about Jamie out of you?'

His fingers were slipping up her spine now, flushing her skin with heat. 'Don't be ridiculous,' she snapped.

'But it's working so well,' he said softly, pulling her close as the curtain dropped away. 'Isn't this just what you had in mind?'

'No,' she gasped. 'You should know how I feel about you, better than anyone.'

'Such flattery,' he said admiringly, his fingers trailing across her throat and down the curve of her breasts. 'Did you learn it out of one of those self-help books that you have so many of in your flat?'

'Stop it,' she whispered, her fingers catching at his.

'I don't think those are quite the right words,' he said softly, his lips coming down on hers. 'Perhaps you turned over two pages at once.'

'Jake, I—' But the words she had been going to say died as his lips met hers and her hands slid inexorably up his chest.

She had thought once that her feelings for Jake were just part of a sort of teenage madness. Overwhelming at the time, but as the years went by, meant to become over and forgotten.

The fact that she simply couldn't forget those feelings, however hard she tried, was something that in the end she had simply had to accept. She had done her best to avoid Jake, but the knowledge of him had always stayed in her heart.

Now as she responded hungrily to his searching mouth and then felt the faint rasp of his unshaven chin against her throat, she knew with blinding clarity that her emotions were veering out of control.

Jake's eyes were boring down into her very soul, his fingers searching out an answering need as they swept down her damp body.

But what could she possibly mean to him, except as someone who had answers that he wanted? It was obvious he despised everything about her. Summoning the remaining shreds of her self-control, she reached blindly for the shower taps and twirled them full on.

The sudden blast of water took him as much by surprise as it had her a few moments earlier. She smiled sweetly up into his face, the water plastering his dark hair to his head and sluicing down his shirt collar. 'What's the matter?' she inquired as steadily as she could. 'Don't you expect to get wet when you step into a shower?'

He pulled away from her, his eyes as black as a winter's night. 'I guess I don't expect to have to share it with a she-devil,' he said coldly.

She shook herself away from him and, grabbing a towel, wrapped it hurriedly around herself. 'You're just sore because you expect every woman you meet to fall over backwards for you. Must be quite a jolt to your ego to realize you simply don't turn me on at all.'

He stared at her assessingly for a moment and then, putting two fingers down the front of her towel, drew her slowly to him. 'Do you realize how devastated you make me feel with that brilliant analysis of my ego and your emotions?'

Sara swallowed. 'It's true,' she spat defiantly.

'Uh-huh,' he replied, bending to kiss her once more. His lips were gentle, coaxing, and Sara, after one shuddering second, responded with all the hungry need that her body had ever known.

Then as her hands crept around his neck, he pulled away, and her eyes fluttered open to see him staring at her, outwardly calm, but the pulse in his neck throbbing with wild intensity.

'What's the matter?' she breathed, hardly knowing what she was saying.

He shrugged, a bitter little smile on his face. 'Nothing,' he drawled. 'Except that I'm devastated at your obvious distaste for me.'

'You—' she began, but he was too quick for her.

'Save it,' he interrupted. 'I guess we're both in the wrong. But let me give you a piece of advice, Sara.'

'What?' she asked unthinkingly.

He reached for the door handle and turned back to look at her. 'Next time you tell someone how unaffected you are by them, you'd be wise to switch the shower off before you wrap yourself in a towel.'

CHAPTER SIX

SARA soaped her hair angrily for several minutes after he had left, muttering several suggestions, all of them biologically impossible, which she should have made to Jake. Blast the man! What right had he to make her feel like this? And, moreover, to make such blatant fun of her feelings? She would show him.

Several minutes later, and still seething, she got out of the shower and dried herself off with the only other towel in the room. It was obviously meant for Jake's use, and it was only the last minute realization of how childish she would seem that stopped her from hurling it into the shower and giving it a thorough soaking. She couldn't remember ever being so angry. How dare he swan back into her life and churn her up like this?

Pulling on a clean pair of jeans and a crisp white cotton shirt, practically the only things, apart from her underwear, that Jake had not chucked into the airport litter bin, she walked back into the bedroom, her head high, ready for battle.

But Jake was not there.

Her hair was almost dry by the time he returned and there was a smile on his face that made it difficult to pick up the conversation where he had so devastatingly left it. 'Jake—' she began determinedly.

But he was too quick for her. 'Great news, Sara. Guess what?'

Taken aback by his cheerfulness, she could only stare in amazement at him. He threw himself on the bed and smiled up at her, for all the world like a big cat that had just had a particularly good day's hunting.

'I can't imagine,' she said acidly. 'What?'

He looked at her more closely and then shook his head. 'Oh dear, still sulking, I see.'

'I am not sulking!' she snapped.

His lips twitched. 'Guess I've stolen your thunder, hmm?'

She lifted her chin and looked pointedly away from him. 'I don't know what you mean,' she said primly.

'Oh, I think you do,' Jake replied softly. 'I bet you thought of at least five really searing things to say to me when you came out of the shower. I expect they were really good, too. Full of hell-fire and especially designed to turn me into a small heap of shivering ash for daring to so upset your natural dignity.'

'I wouldn't lower myself to bandy insults with you,' Sara remarked loftily, secretly aghast at how he could read her so accurately.

This time, to her utter fury, he laughed out loud.

'Don't you dare laugh at me, you rotten swine,' she hissed. 'I may only be a showbiz reporter, but at least I'm a good one. I bet you only became a war photographer because nobody'd dare complain that your pictures were out of focus. You could just come up with some incredibly macho excuse like you'd been rattled by mortar fire or something.'

Jake gazed at her, the amusement only too evident on his strong features. 'My pictures are never out of focus,' he said silkily. 'But since you are so obviously convinced that they are, maybe you should think about wearing glasses. You know, the sort that are made of bottle bottoms.'

'Maybe I should get the bottles from those hard-drinking cronies of yours,' she retorted. 'Then I'd be bound to get a really wide selection. And I'd certainly never run out.'

In answer, Jake pulled her down onto the bed and leaned over her. Her pulse seemed to be going ten to the dozen and she swallowed hard as she saw the expression on his face.

'What's the matter?' she demanded, with more bravery than she felt. 'Found that you can dish it out, but you just can't take it?'

His face was only a few inches from hers now, his eyes searing into hers. 'You can insult me as much as you like, Sara,' he said, every word clear in the silent room. 'But I would be grateful if you didn't apply your overly fertile imagination to slinging mud at my friends. One of them died last week, taking some of those pictures that you despise so much.'

Their eyes locked, but Sara's were the first to look away.

'I'm sorry,' she muttered.

A few seconds that seemed like years elapsed and then Jake sighed and rolled over onto his back. 'It's all right,' he said grimly. 'I didn't exactly expect to get on with you on this trip.'

'Well, you haven't exactly made things easy for me,' Sara replied tartly, stung more deeply than she would have liked to admit by his obviously still-low opinion of her.

She stared at the ceiling for a few moments and then turned on her side to face him. His eyes were closed, his body still, almost as if he were unconscious.

'Jake?' she said uncertainly.

'Hmm?' He opened his eyes and glanced sidewise at her. 'What is it? Got any shiny new insults you want to try out on me?'

Sara shook her head. 'Not yet,' she retorted icily, still so easily stung by his taunting. 'I'm still at the polishing stage.' She paused and then added more steadily, 'You said when you came in that you had some good news.'

'So I did,' he murmured sleepily.

'Well?' she demanded, sitting up. 'What is it?'

'Oh, nothing much,' he said, punching his pillow and turning onto his side. 'Except that I've managed to hire a driver and transport to take us into town this afternoon.'

'I still don't understand how you managed this,' Sara said as she and Jake bumped around on the back seat of a dilapidated car, which jolted unsteadily into the city a few hours later.

He shrugged. 'It was probably the simplest thing I've ever done,' he replied.

'But how?' she repeated. 'Why aren't there boatloads of soldiers after us?'

'Sara,' he began, 'what is green and all-powerful?'

'I don't know,' she said, exasperated at his obliqueness. 'American Express? Brussels sprouts? Emperor Ming of Mong?'

He grinned at her. 'Close. Try U.S. dollars. It's amazing what they can do for you when you're in a tight spot.'

'You mean bribery?' yelped Sara. 'You're mad! We're bound to be arrested before you can say Uncle Sam.'

His hand closed over hers. 'It's not bribery. And we're not doing anything wrong. We're just going to visit a couple of temples and see if we can get some pictures. I made damn sure I told the man at reception where we were going. Laid it on really thick how we loved the scenery and all the local colour. He didn't seem to mind at all, and when I slipped him some money, he fixed up the taxi. If we're stopped, we just play up the innocent honeymooners' image.'

'You're mad,' breathed Sara. 'Stark, staring—'

'Sara,' he interrupted grimly, 'save it. We're here on a job, remember? And we are going to get this story no matter what.'

The crowds were such that the car was forced to slow down as they went past the burned-out depot, and Jake, using his tiny camera, again managed to get off a few shots of the wreckage.

Looking about her, Sara noted the numbers of troops on the streets, how they were armed, and the faces of the ordinary people, shuttered by suspicion.

No one seemed to pay the slightest attention to Jake and Sara, as if they had as little part to play in the looming unrest as the occasional plane that screamed overhead.

The deeper they got into town, the closer Sara moved to Jake, her hand instinctively reaching for his, her overstretched nerves needing the comfort that only his closeness could provide.

And however he felt about her, however much he despised her lifestyle and thought the worst of her for lying about Jamie's death, he seemed to know that now was a time to put all this aside.

But he would probably never know, she thought with a lurch of her heart, exactly how much she would always owe him for this one brief interlude, where she could pretend, however fleetingly, that they were close once more.

The car stopped at the top of a street lined with stalls and leading down to the main food market. Jake looked at her assessingly, his fingers reaching out briefly to touch her cheek. 'Ready?' he asked.

She nodded. 'As I'll ever be.'

He smiled. 'Come on, then. Let's go and be tourists.'

Half the stalls were empty, Sara noticed, but there were plenty loaded with bales of material and pots and pans, as if the people who owned them had decided that life would go on. Come hell or high water. 'More likely hell,' murmured Sara to herself, frustrated by the fact that no one seemed to know any English at all.

'You'll just have to use your eyes,' Jake told her, almost as if he could read her mind. 'It's far too dangerous to even attempt to talk to anyone about anything but shopping.'

'Danger never put you off doing anything,' retorted Sara.

'Dangerous for them, not you,' Jake replied with searing simplicity.

Reddening, she plunged down the street to a stall selling brightly coloured scarves and, more to occupy her mind than anything else, began bargaining.

A small crowd soon gathered around and stood laughing at the stallholder's attempts to push up his prices, while Sara, with all the determination of a bargain hunter in the January sales, showed him in perfect dumb show what she thought of his merchandise.

A few minutes later, he threw up his arms in mock resignation and dumped a ten-foot length of striped wool into her arms. Sara, feeling guilty about how earnestly she had thrown herself into beating him down, handed over the few coins he wanted and was deeply relieved to see him beam at the clapping crowd.

'Great piece of investigative journalism,' Jake told her grimly as they continued down the street.

'I had to do something,' she forced out. 'All this pretence is getting on my nerves.'

There was silence, but his voice when he spoke was deceptively mild. 'Interesting idea,' he observed. 'Shopping as curative medicine. Perhaps it should be on the National Health.'

'Perhaps it should,' replied Sara, refusing at last to be baited. 'Women have known for centuries how soothing the process is.'

'Especially when they can get somebody else to pay,' drawled Jake.

Sara's lips tightened. 'Of course,' she gritted.

He looked at her sideways. 'Well, well,' he observed, 'this must be the first time I've failed to wind you up.'

'I'm not a clock, Jake,' she replied sweetly. 'I just decided you were right. We have to work together, so we might as well be pleasant to each other.'

Jake's eyebrows rose and he turned to face her. He moved so suddenly she bumped into him, and he reached out to steady her. 'You know,' he said quietly, 'I thought I knew all about you, and yet you continually surprise me.'

He was far too close, and the pressure of his hand on her arm was flooding her skin with heat. 'Do I?' she forced out, searching his face hopelessly for a softness, a way he once had of looking at her. 'Is that good?'

His fingers lifted to brush her cheek. 'It means that I'm continually wondering where I was right and where I was wrong about you,' he admitted.

'I'm not as bad as you keep telling me I am,' she said in a low voice, her heart filled with a sudden wild longing.

'Really?' he said softly, leaning down to kiss her.

Her whole body jolted at the contact. He shouldn't affect her like this. He shouldn't. Not after all these years. In confusion she pulled away. 'I can't,' she whispered. 'You—'

He straightened abruptly, a bitter look in his eyes. 'What, Sara?' he demanded. 'What name were you going to call me this time?'

'I wasn't—' she burst out in surprise.

'Save it,' he cut in wearily. 'It's not worth the argument.' Then something in his expression changed, and grabbing Sara by the hand, he set off purposefully up the street.

'What's the matter?' she said breathlessly, half-running to keep up with his long strides.

He slowed his pace and gazed down at her for a moment. 'We're being followed,' he said shortly, 'by that appalling man from the so-called Government Tourist Agency.'

'What?' she gasped, stifling the urge to look behind her.

'He's about ten feet away,' he told her. 'Just keep walking and smiling and we'll go and have a look round this temple just up here on the right. He has to believe we're nothing but harmless tourists.'

The temple was dim after the stark brightness of the day outside, and it reverberated to the continuous low chanting from lines of monks kneeling on the floor.

The atmosphere was such that Sara hesitated on the threshold, but Jake pulled her forward. 'Come on,' he urged in a whisper. 'No one minds our being here as long as we show some respect.'

Her hand slid easily into his as they threaded their way around the walls and out into a sunny courtyard. 'Look,' breathed Sara. 'There's that monk again.'

Coming towards them was the monk who had so carefully inspected their hotel bedroom. His face split into a huge grin, and Sara couldn't help smiling back.

He bowed to Jake and she was astonished to see the way Jake also gravely inclined his head. 'Well, well,' she whispered, 'that must be a first. The proud Jake Armstrong showing some respect to somebody.'

He opened his mouth, but any retort that he was going to make was silenced by the monk turning to Sara and holding out his hand. A small toffee lay on his palm, and he nodded encouragingly at her.

She picked it up in bewilderment and looked at Jake. 'What am I supposed to do now?' she muttered. 'Put it on some altar, or what?'

Jake shrugged. 'Eat it,' he suggested. 'It's a sweet, isn't it?'

'I might offend him,' Sara returned through clenched teeth. 'It could be an offering of some sort.' The monk stood back still smiling at her encouragingly and obviously waiting for her to act. 'Jake,' she pleaded, 'what do I do?'

But the monk took matters into his own hands. Opening his mouth slowly, he pointed to it as if instructing a backward child, and Sara, with a gasp of relief, unwrapped the sweet and popped it into her mouth.

'It's brilliant toffee,' she mumbled indistinctly and was rewarded by peals of laughter from the monk.

'You're undoubtedly his star pupil,' Jake remarked drily.

'At least somebody in this place is willing to believe I like to act for the best,' countered Sara. 'Unlike you.'

Jake opened his mouth to reply, but Lama Banideya was pointing at Jake's shirt pocket now, where he kept his miniature camera, and after a moment's hesitation, Jake pulled it out to show him.

As if by lightning, the monk's long brown fingers closed over it and it seemed to disappear up his sleeve as Sara and Jake were hailed from the temple doorway.

It was the man from the Government Tourist Agency. 'I see you are enjoying the sights of our wonderful historic and holy city,' he boomed, bowing his head at them.

This time, Jake did not return the compliment, but stood silent, watchful as their jailer swaggered towards them.

'Perhaps I did not make it clear that there are guided tours available if you wish to visit the city,' he continued. 'It is very dangerous for you to be walking here alone. Anything could happen and we would not be responsible.'

'Oh, yes, you would,' murmured Jake.

Sara could see the barely controlled tension in his face, and grabbed his arm. 'I'm sorry if we've done anything wrong,' she gabbled pleadingly. 'But we did so want to have a look round before we went home. It is a truly beautiful city, and a once-in-a-lifetime experience.'

The man gazed at them assessingly and then held out his hand. 'I can understand that,' he nodded. 'But I am going to have to ask you for your camera.'

A ghost of a smile crossed Jake's face. 'I'm afraid I can't help you there,' he said seriously. 'We know how sensitive everything is at the moment, so we left it at the hotel.'

The man's face darkened and he stared angrily at them both for a moment. 'Turn out your pockets,' he ordered Jake.

Without batting an eyelid, Jake slowly did as he was told, smiling calmly at the man.

'It's a wonder that penknife hasn't worn a hole through your trousers,' remarked Sara as she saw the little pile of possessions mount up on the ground.

'Such housewifely concern,' drawled Jake. 'You never fail to surprise me.'

But the man was looking furiously at Sara now. 'Empty your handbag,' he told her.

'My handbag?' she echoed.

'Come on, Sara,' Jake said impatiently, stuffing his possessions back into his pockets. 'This is no time for your Lady Bracknell impersonation. Empty it out.'

'This is ridiculous,' she gritted, before crouching down and upending her bag over the dusty ground.

A stream of tissues, pens, loose change, spare tights, lipsticks and some fluff-infested chocolate poured over the floor. Both men peered at the pile. 'No camera there,' remarked Jake, his long fingers sifting through the little heap before lighting on a piece of paper with Sara's name scrawled on it. 'This is Jamie's writing,' he said, whisking it out of her reach.

'Give it back,' she pleaded, lunging for it. 'It's a private letter.' But it was no good. He had already begun to read it, his face darkening.

'Pack up your things,' snarled their guard. 'I will take that paper.' And snatching it from Jake's fingers, he turned on his heel. 'Be so good as to follow me. Your car is waiting outside to take you back to the hotel.'

Jake, his eyes glittering with fury, looked at Sara. 'You heard the man,' he said softly. 'Better get packed up.'

Swearing under her breath, Sara swept her possessions back into her handbag and stood up. But before she stepped back into the dimness of the temple, she looked back over her shoulder at the sunny courtyard. Of Lama Banideya, there was no sign.

This time they were escorted all the way back to their bedroom instead of just being dropped in reception, and Sara distinctly heard the rasp of the key in the lock as the door was closed on them.

She sat limply in the bed and looked tentatively at Jake. 'How much of that letter did you read?' she forced out.

'Enough to know that my worst suspicions were true,' he grated. 'I'm surprised you kept it. Even you're not heartless enough to want to gloat over it. Or are you?'

'You can't have read it all,' she replied desperately. 'You've obviously just got the wrong end of the stick.'

'"Don't do this to me, Sara,"' quoted Jake with brutal accuracy. '"How can you be so cold when you know it means so much to me?"' He stared at her. 'I would have thought what Jamie wrote was fairly self-explanatory.'

'It's not what you think,' she whispered. 'Please, Jake, maybe we can ask that man to give the letter back and then you can see for yourself that it's not what you think.'

'The idea of his giving anything back is pretty unlikely,' snarled Jake. 'And I expect you're banking on that.'

'No,' pleaded Sara, 'I'm not. Now you've seen part of that letter, maybe I should tell you everything. Please listen.'

'Maybe not,' he said flatly. 'And I should have known better than to expect the truth from you. All you're going to give me is a pack of lies. Jamie loved you, and all you wanted from him was his money.'

'That's not true!' she burst out.

'Don't lie to me,' snapped Jake. 'Don't you think I've been through Jamie's things? Don't you think I've seen his cheque-books, with all those stubs made out to you, or Aspreys or some other Bond Street shop where he spent all his money on you?'

She gazed at him pleadingly. 'It's not true, Jake. I swear it. If only you'd listen—'

'I'm past listening,' he ground out. 'And I'm past caring about you.'

There was a small silence. 'You never did anyway,' Sara said at last. 'Maybe once long ago when we were growing up. But then you left. And since that time you haven't cared about anyone except yourself.'

Jake gave her one burning look and swung away to the window. The atmosphere was so tense she almost expected him to put his fist through it. But instead, he gazed out at the mountains, a muscle in his cheek going like a steam hammer.

Finally he turned to face her, his face grim. 'Let's get one thing straight, shall we?' he said curtly. 'I don't like you, and you don't like me. But if we're going to get out of this in one piece, then unfortunately we are going to have to bury our differences, at least for the present.'

'How irritating for you,' snapped Sara. 'When we both know you'd much rather be burying me.'

'How right you are,' he retorted, and she shivered at his tone. All the lightness that had crept back into his treatment of her had evaporated. An assignment she had begun in rather a perverse way to enjoy, simply because of his presence, had now turned in seconds into a cold, cold nightmare.

Desperately she gazed at him, hoping against hope that his eyes would soften. But they remained as hard and unforgiving as wet granite.

'I don't know about teamwork,' she said at last. 'You're the one who blew a lot of hard cash on a taxi that should have been pensioned off thirty years ago. And for what? We spend the entire afternoon being followed by someone who is patently a graduate of the Spanish Inquisition, you get your camera stolen, and now we're locked in our room instead of having the run of the hotel.'

Jake stepped towards her and she flinched involuntarily, but he flopped down in an armchair and gazed

at the ceiling. 'Well, no wonder you're upset,' he
drawled. 'Now you're locked in, you obviously won't
be able to swan down to the beauty parlour and spend
your expenses on Bandhul's latest designer dresses.'

'Ha ha,' Sara retorted coldly, throwing herself face
down on her pillow.

A sudden shift in the mattress told her he was on the
bed, and her whole body stilled. His hand grasped her
shoulder and he pushed her onto her side to face him.

'I don't know why you're so upset,' he said roughly.
'It wasn't your camera, and you didn't shell out for the
taxi, but now you've got plenty of background stuff for
a good colour piece when we eventually get out of here.
Because if we hadn't made the effort this afternoon, we
would have been sent home with a flea in our ears and
not much to write about.'

'I don't give a stuff about this job any more,' she said
stormily. 'You saw all the same things today as I did.
You write the story.'

'Don't be so childish,' he grated.

'I'm not being childish,' she protested.

'Then you're doing a pretty good impression of it,'
Jake replied roughly. 'You look like you did on your
eleventh birthday when I offered you a ride on my horse
and you were almost too frightened to get on, but you
did—simply because you wouldn't admit how you felt.'

Sara swallowed. I must not, must not, cry, she told
herself sternly. 'I was not—' she choked out abruptly.

Jake's finger traced a path down her cheek-bone to
her chin. 'Are they real tears?' he inquired. 'Or crocodile
ones?'

'Why so surprised at the idea they might be genuine,'
she muttered, 'when you spend all your time hounding
me about Jamie?'

He rounded on her furiously. 'Leave him out of this, OK? Just for once in your life, take the blame for your own actions.'

'But Jamie—' she tried again, a desperate note in her voice.

He glanced at her impatiently. 'Don't bring Jamie into this. I don't know why I even brought up the subject, except that now, years after I thought I'd become completely immune to what was clearly a passing attraction, I have to admit I'm still intrigued by you.'

'A passing attraction?' she whispered.

'Even you can't have forgotten what happened,' he grated.

'Forgotten?' she echoed. 'I remember that night as well as you do. I don't think I could ever forget it.'

Her mind's eye looked back, back to the high grass in the orchard and the blossom falling on her face, as though it had come all the way from the dark midnight sky.

There was silence, then she sighed and looked wearily at Jake. 'I thought you loved me, you know. Silly, really, I suppose, but I don't think I've ever got over it.'

'It was a mistake,' he said coldly.

'Obviously,' she said sadly. 'You went away the next day, before I woke up. You didn't even bother to say goodbye.'

'We were too young,' he said grimly. 'It was better that way.'

She stared at him. 'Who for, Jake?' she asked softly. 'You or me?'

He made an impatient gesture with his hands and then let out a long breath. 'I don't know why I'm bothering to tell you this, Sara, considering everything that's happened, but every emotion in me made me want, to stay after that night, to be with you.

'But I thought it wouldn't be fair. I was twenty-four years old and you were seventeen. Still a child, really.' He shrugged helplessly. 'I should have known better than to make love to you that night. It should never have happened.'

'You disliked me that much?' whispered Sara.

He shook his head in disbelief. 'Disliked?' he echoed. 'Never that, Sara. Not then. I just felt that I'd robbed you of something. You gave yourself to me so freely, so—' He stopped abruptly. 'You were too young, that's all. And I took advantage.'

'Is that an apology, then?' she asked, trying hard to sound flippant, unhurt.

He grabbed her arm and pulled her to him. 'Do you know how much it cost me to go?' he grated. 'If I'd gone to say goodbye to you, I'd never have left. But you were only seventeen. I can't tell you how guilty I felt. I thought it was unfair of me to make any claim on you. You were just too young.'

'You didn't even leave a note,' she accused.

'Of course I left you a note,' he said impatiently. 'I gave it to Jamie.'

Her lips parted. 'I never got it,' she whispered.

'Just like you never got that plane ticket I sent you when I couldn't stand being without you any longer,' he grated.

She stared at him wordlessly, the years rolling back. And Jamie, smiling Jamie, at the centre of it all.

'You really did love me, didn't you?' she whispered at last.

He made an impatient movement with his hand. 'What does it matter now,' he said roughly, 'when I know for a fact how you treated Jamie?'

She felt as if her heart had been cut out and dropped in freezing water. 'It's not true,' she denied.

He stared grimly at her. 'Still lying to yourself, I see.'

'Jake,' she pleaded urgently, 'you must listen to me.'

'I must?' he asked contemptuously.

'But there's so much to explain,' she said in a rush. 'And you have to tell me—'

Jake shrugged irritably. 'I don't have to tell you anything, and I certainly don't want your explanations. Can't you see that it's years too late? It's best written off as just a teenage thing. Madness. Absolute meaningless madness.'

Sara jerked a blanket over her shoulders. 'And I thought I was supposed to be the one who was self-indulgent and silly,' she mocked.

'Now wait just a minute—' he began.

'No, Jake,' she interrupted. 'It's been seven and a half years, and I'm not going to wait any longer. Yes, I was only a teenager then. Seventeen and ten months on that night. But it didn't matter to me how old either of us was. Do you know how much you hurt me, just going off like that without a word?'

'I didn't leave you without a word,' he insisted. 'But as I keep telling you, if I'd seen you again that morning, I would never have gone. I only realized how much you truly meant to me when I got to Australia. I worked night and day to get the money to pay for that ticket. And do you know how much it hurt *me* to get it back like that?'

'But—' she began.

He sighed. 'Leave it, Sara. You've already told me once. It's just ridiculous stirring up old feelings like this. We both know it's over. None of it matters now.'

'I thought you'd deserted me,' she said bitterly. 'Lucky for me I wasn't pregnant.'

He shook her shoulder. 'Don't you think I didn't worry about that, too? I didn't know what to do. I asked Jamie to keep an eye on you, I told you in the letter with the ticket...' He stopped and ran a hand through his hair. 'You know I would have come straight back if anything had happened.'

'Of course,' she muttered dully.

Jake slipped his hand from her shoulder and sighed. 'Even if it's true that Jamie destroyed my letter and tore up the ticket—because that's the only reasonable explanation—it doesn't really change anything now. As far as you were concerned, he was in love with you and you still treated him like dirt.'

'It wasn't like that,' said Sara. 'You just don't know how betrayed I felt when I found you'd gone without even saying goodbye. I thought—' she swallowed '—I thought you despised me.'

'We were too young, Sara,' he said more gently. 'It would have ended in disaster.'

She bit her lip. 'Ever since I arrived at your house, I looked up to you, hero-worshipped you, if you like. You were always so brilliant to me, and then...I fell in love with you.' She swallowed hard. 'And when you left, I thought you must hate me. You never even wrote.' Jake gestured impatiently, but she carried on in a low voice. 'Since this trip began, all those feelings have come back.' Sara looked down at the floor. 'I just can't deny how I feel about you, Jake,' she choked out. 'I can't and God knows I've tried.'

'Do you really still remember that night?' he demanded.

A tear slid from her eye, and she dashed it away with the back of her hand. 'Yes,' she muttered.

'You surprise me,' he said quietly. 'I thought you would have forgotten it by now, seeing as it was eight years ago.'

'Seven and a half,' she corrected.

He smiled wryly and sighed. 'You're like two entirely different people, Sara. And the trouble is I never know which one I'm going to get when I talk to you. It's like dealing with a split personality.'

'Is that your expert medical opinion?' she grated.

'Look at it from my point of view,' Jake began.

'No,' she bit out. 'I don't want to. Just for once in my life it would be nice for you to believe that I'm acting out of honourable motives instead of being hounded incessantly to tell you everything about Jamie. Why do you have to be the judge and jury about my decisions?'

His face darkened. 'If I thought you were "honourable", then maybe I wouldn't hound you,' he ground out. 'But since you treated Jamie so abominably, why shouldn't I know the truth?'

'I didn't treat him abominably,' she countered. 'You're just so wrong about me.'

His eyes hardened. 'Prove it.'

She glared at him. 'I hate you, Jake.'

He smiled bitterly. 'There you go again, Sara. Two entirely opposing statements in less than five minutes. And you ask me why I simply can't believe anything you say?'

She stared at him, unshed tears welling in her eyes. 'There isn't anything I can say that will change your mind, is there?' she muttered.

'No,' he said simply.

She dashed her hand once more against her eyes. 'You're right,' she said at last, trying hard to sound business-like as her heart began to splinter for the second time in her life. 'We have to think about here and now.'

He nodded. 'I'm glad you agree,' he drawled.

'It's just that now we're locked in and those men could come back at any minute, and frankly—' She stopped short.

'Frankly what?' he said quietly.

She glanced up at him and could bear it no longer. 'I'm scared, Jake,' she blurted out, a sob breaking in her throat. 'Absolutely bloody petrified, if you must know.'

CHAPTER SEVEN

MORE than anything, Sara wanted the feel of Jake's arms around her, and yet it was the last thing in the world that she could have. She swallowed desperately.

She looked at the shadows below Jake's eyes, the pallor of his skin beneath his tan, and thought for the first time of the pressure he was under.

She had been nothing, really, but a dead weight on his back ever since they'd arrived in this God-forsaken place. 'I'm sorry, Jake,' she muttered.

'So am I,' he said simply. 'I had hoped to get some sense out of you about Jamie and lay the past to rest. But all we've done is wear our emotions to shreds.'

'You mean you wanted me to live down to your expectations,' she accused fiercely. 'You wanted to go away happy in the knowledge that I was every bit as silly and vain and shallow as you had decided I was.'

He stared at her blankly. 'Something like that, yes, if you like,' he said wearily. 'Who cares now anyway?'

Scrubbing violently at her swollen eyelids, she sat up on the bed and raked her fingers through her hair. 'I do,' she forced out.

He opened his mouth to reply, but a key rattled in the lock and they both stilled, Jake reaching out a hand to her. But before he could say anything, the door was thrown open and the man from the tourist agency walked into the room. 'Good evening,' he said, smiling.

Standing in the middle of their bedroom, he looked such an incongruous figure in his neat blue suit, his mirrored sunglasses reflecting Sara's startled face. But there was no doubt that the menace behind his amiable expression was only too real.

'I don't see what's good about it,' drawled Jake. 'Close the door on your way out, why don't you?'

Their jailer stepped up to the foot of the bed. 'So nice to see honeymooners in such obvious harmony.' He leered unpleasantly.

As assured as a big cat, Jake levered himself off the bed and padded up to the man, who stepped back hurriedly. 'You got something to say?' Jake inquired lazily.

The man clenched his jaw. 'I want to take your camera away for examination,' he grated. 'You know,' he added silkily, 'the one you said you left here while you went on your so-called sightseeing trip this afternoon.'

'But—' began Sara, subsiding at a warning look from Jake.

'Sure,' he said with a shrug. 'Why not?' Opening his case, he took out a normal-sized 35mm camera and handed it over. 'Anything else?' he added. 'Money? Western clothes? Or maybe even our addresses so your kid sister can spend the summer with us improving her English?'

The man grabbed the camera and glared at Jake. 'That will be all,' he snapped and left the room, the key once more loudly turning in the lock.

'Wow,' breathed Sara. 'You certainly have a talent for diplomacy, don't you?'

'Can't possibly be any worse than your talent for journalism,' Jake drawled.

She swung her legs over the edge of the bed. 'At least I've got all the information I've gathered up here,' she said, tapping her head.

'Good place for it,' he said idly, 'considering you don't keep much else up there.'

'You can make your cheap cracks,' snapped Sara. 'But I'm not the one who's now had two cameras stolen in one afternoon.'

'I may have had the cameras stolen,' he gritted. 'But I've still got most of the film I shot. What do you take me for?'

He stepped towards her and she bit her lip at the expression on his face.

'Haven't you even stopped to think how incredibly lucky we were that that monk took our first camera?' he demanded. 'If our friend from the tourist agency had got his hands on the film in that, you can bet your bottom dollar we wouldn't be lounging about in here now.'

'You're exaggerating,' Sara said with a firmness she didn't feel. 'How do you know he's not just trying to keep us out of trouble? He could be doing exactly what he says he is and protecting us from getting hurt.'

Jake gave her a withering look. 'Do me a favour,' he said coldly.

'I agree he's a bit heavy-handed,' she protested. 'But we don't know enough to judge exactly what he's up to.'

'Listen, Sara,' Jake began impatiently. 'I'll tell you exactly what's going through that nasty, suspicious little mind of his. We are a couple of ignorant-seeming westerners who have barged into his country at exactly the wrong time. There's going to be a bloody great rebellion here sooner rather than later, and we are right slap-bang in the way.'

He breathed in deeply and then, striding to the window, continued, 'At the moment, it seems that as long as we act ignorantly and do the outraged-tourist bit, we'll be all right. With a bit of luck, we'll be sent on our way just like every other westerner he said was in this hotel until a few days ago.

'It was bloody lucky I brought that other camera, because now it means that our cover story is backed up. But if he has the slightest evidence to show that we're not who we say we are, then the best we could hope for would be a long sentence in some jail that makes our last room look like the penthouse suite at the Dorchester.'

He turned to face her, his body a black silhouette against the brightness of the sky. 'If you value your life at all, you'll stop worrying about the loss of a lousy camera and start hoping they will stick to their word and fly us out of here.'

'Of course they're going to fly us out,' retorted Sara, and then as Jake gazed in silence at her, added falteringly, 'Are-n't they?'

His lips twisted into a bitter smile. 'You have such a touching faith in humanity, Sara.'

'But they must,' she whispered, appalled at the horrific avenue of thought opening up in her brain.

'Why should they?' he demanded. 'If we prove too much trouble, we're just a pair of obscure honeymooners who could quite easily disappear here without a ripple.'

'But you're a powerful man,' objected Sara. 'You must be able to pull some strings.'

Jake looked at her wearily. 'What odds would you give for our survival if they knew what we did for a living?' he asked. 'Think about it, Sara. Journalism has long been equated with spying in this part of the world, and since we had to come under false pretences, the truth will come to look so much blacker against us if they find out who we really are.

'Whichever way we look, we're trapped. For the moment, as long as they believe our story, we have to stick to it and hope for the best.'

Sara had the sudden feeling that she was falling very fast down a very long lift shaft. 'You . . . you don't think they might...they might actually kill us?' she stammered.

He shrugged. 'I don't know,' he said simply. 'I hope not. Our only policy must be to appear absolutely straight, or we're done for.'

Sara nervously clasped and unclasped her hands and then looked at Jake. 'Isn't there anything we can do?' she said at last.

He shrugged. 'Well, I don't know about you,' he drawled. 'But I'm going to have a shower.'

'Shower?' she repeated incredulously.

Jake nodded slowly. 'Yes. Not without its risks, I agree, but I'll try to live up to your standards of bravery in dealing with the unexpected.' He smiled slowly down into her narrowing eyes and went into the bathroom.

Sara stood for a few minutes, hands clenched while her mind desperately searched for a caustic retort that would finally put him in his place. Unable to find one at all, she shrugged angrily and turning on her heel looked once more around the room.

It was much nicer than the room they had spent their first night in, she had to concede, but had become their prison none the less. The door, under her probing hand, felt all too solid and was definitely firmly locked.

The cupboards, too, seemed as though they were going to yield nothing of any help whatsoever, until she opened the last one and gasped in astonishment. For it was not a cupboard at all, but a small, concealed refrigerator, and inside, its dark green glass beaded with condensation, was a bottle of champagne.

Her hand closed wonderingly around her prize, and lifting it out, she sat back on the bed.

* * *

The pop of the cork sounded just like a bullet, she thought, as the pale gold liquid creamed into their tin mugs. She took a sip and then raised her head to see Jake standing in the bathroom doorway, a towel round his slim hips, with an expression on his face that could freeze blood.

'What the hell do you thin you're doing?' he demanded, his thick, dark eyebrows drawing together in one angry line as he stalked towards her and picked up the bottle.

'Opening some champagne I found,' she replied defensively, and then as he continued to scowl at her, added defiantly, 'Why, what did you think I was doing?'

He put the bottle down on the bedside table, a weary expression overcoming his anger. 'God knows,' he sighed, shaking his head. 'I guess I shouldn't be surprised if I walked in here and found you roller-skating with the Abominable Snowman.'

'It's only a bottle of champagne,' she objected.

'So I see,' he drawled. 'Since it's the honeymoon suite, what else should there be in it except champagne?' He glanced at the label. 'And an expensive French variety to boot. Shame there's no food to go with it.'

Sara glared at him. 'Why don't you just ring room service?' she said tartly. 'You could ask them to send up some eggs Benedict and a couple of bowls of strawberries.'

'What a good idea,' he snarled. 'And maybe even a brain replacement, seeing as yours has obviously just seized up completely.'

'That's an appalling way to speak to anyone,' breathed Sara. 'Least of all the only friend you've got in the biggest mess you've ever been in.'

'With friends like you—' began Jake. Then stopping suddenly, he sat on the bed and looked at her. 'This isn't some hooray party in Chelsea, you know,' he said slightly more gently. 'The last thing we need at the moment is alcohol.'

'We're locked up,' remonstrated Sara, raising the mug once more to her lips and taking an extra large mouthful, mentally daring him to stop her as the bubbles exploded on her tongue. 'And we're both tired and irritable. I thought it would just be a bit of fun. Something to cheer us up.'

He sighed. 'We're feeling so rotten mainly because we are at this very high altitude, and we haven't yet acclimatized properly. It can take a week for your lungs to get used to the air here. You've only had a handful of walnuts and some yoghurt to eat today. And drinking, especially champagne, is only going to make you feel worse.'

'Well, I don't feel worse at all,' Sara replied loftily, her head suddenly reeling. 'I feel absomarvelly luteless.'

'So I see,' Jake said drily, taking the mug from her unresisting fingers.

'Tell you one thing,' she said hazily, gazing owlishly at him. 'That bottle would be brilliant for beaning that man from the Government Tourist Agency.'

'Why don't you call him in?' drawled Jake. 'And then when you've got him to stand with his back to us, I'll put your theory to the test.'

Without even realizing it, Sara's fingers curled around his. 'Would you like to know something?' she said slowly.

His lips twisted. 'You got a safe bet for the Derby?'

'No,' she whispered, and then gathering the remains of her courage, stared steadily down at their hands. 'If you must know,' she said in a small voice, 'I feel awful.'

'Good,' he replied, not unkindly. 'Although, since you haven't had that much to drink, you won't feel bad for very long. It's exactly the same as drinking too much on an aeroplane.'

She closed her eyes. 'I wish I was on an aeroplane,' she said mournfully.

'So do I,' he said softly.

'Beast,' she retorted half-heartedly, lifting her hand. His fingers, still entwined with hers, pushed it back on the pillows, and he leaned down to kiss her. 'You're taking advantage,' she murmured, her senses reeling at the contact of his hard body, warm and damp from the shower.

'Of course,' he said softly. 'I'm a beast, remember?'

She lifted a hand to his cheek, a droplet of water sliding between her fingers. There was no way she could resist this man; nor, she suddenly realized as her grogginess began to clear, did she want to.

His hand still cupping her face, he pulled away and lay gazing at her. 'How are you feeling now?' he asked quietly.

'You ask me that?' she whispered, aching to move more closely to him. 'You hate me.'

'Of course I do,' he replied softly.

She drew the quilt to her as if to ward off the misery that was seeping through her bones. 'I was so in love with you when I was seventeen,' she said at last. 'You could make me blush just by looking at me.'

'Still can,' he said, gazing at her steadily.

She could feel the blood rushing to her cheeks as his eyes travelled the length of her body. She put a hand to her throat. Even that felt unnaturally hot. 'Stop it,' she breathed.

As his eyes met hers again, she felt an ache deep in her heart. Why did she have to tell him her feelings? Expose herself to that caustic wit of his? And then the hurt that she had carefully hidden for all these years would begin all over again.

He reached out for her, and she shivered at his touch. 'Don't,' she said fiercely. 'What are you trying to do? Refresh your memory? What's the point?'

His mouth tightened. 'A lot has happened since you were a shy teenager, Sara. I'm surprised you can remember the feelings you had for me.'

'So am I,' she spat. 'When I've had so many other boyfriends to distract me.'

'Including my brother,' he grated.

She sat bolt upright and glared at him. 'I hate you,' she shouted. 'I hate you so much that if those clowns from the Government Tourist Agency came in right at this moment and took you away, I'd probably cheer.'

He grabbed both her arms and pushed her rigid body down onto the bed. 'No, you wouldn't,' he insisted. 'And do you know why?'

She shook her head in spite of herself.

'Because then you wouldn't have an audience any more,' he continued. 'If I went, who would you shout at then? The shower?'

'I hate you,' she repeated stonily.

He kissed her fiercely on the lips. 'You don't sound very convinced,' he said huskily.

'You're the most awful man I know,' she said, struggling, reaching for the shelter of the bedclothes.

He kissed her again, imprisoning her hands. 'Liar.'

She couldn't speak. Everything about him that she had felt and hoped and cried over so long ago came boilingly to the present, and as his fingers relaxed, her arms slid round him.

No matter how he felt about her, how much he obviously despised her, his presence was too much for her to resist.

She could hardly breathe. His back felt so smooth beneath her fingertips as his arms closed about her. And suddenly there seemed to be nothing more important than that Jake should continue to hold her, to slide his fingers over her body, his touch setting alight the bonfire of her heart.

Arching against him, she was barely aware of his releasing the buttons of her shirt, his skin like warm silk against her own. Then, despair stabbing at her heart, she struggled once more.

'Are you trying to fight me, or yourself?' he murmured, his quiet tones belying the dark glitter of passion in his eyes.

Their gazes met and held and then she reached up to him, pulling him close, so close her senses reeled. 'I don't care if you do hate me,' she gasped. 'I just don't care any more.'

'I don't hate you,' he whispered. 'I've wanted you for so long I just can't hold out any longer.' His hands cupped her breasts, his fingers fluttering over their hardening peaks. He shook his head minutely. 'Nothing else seems to matter any more, Sara. Nothing, but you and I.'

She gazed at him mutely, unable to deny the truth of his words. However he felt now, however much he would regret this moment in the future, he would never know just how much he meant to her.

She could not resist him, her fingers trailing down his forearm, loving the way his muscles flexed at her touch. Loving him.

A soft sigh escaping from his lips, he slid his hands along her skin, stripping away her shirt and jeans, pulling her close so that her body was pressed the length of his, savouring her warm flesh.

His fingers followed the curve of her body, as though he knew every soft plane, as though she were the most precious thing on earth, and as she began to shudder helplessly against him, she knew that she could deny this man nothing.

She should struggle, resist, force him to stop. But even as intense delight began to enclose them, she knew that she didn't want him to stop, no matter what it was going to cost her when that fragile world finally shattered.

Already in these brief seconds she was heady with desire, her body aching against the hardening, urgent pressure of his on hers.

He moved away from her slightly, bending his head so that his dark head could caress her breasts, savouring her uncontrolled response, smiling at the little sound she made in her throat.

Her senses spinning, she moved instinctively, her body drowning in a warm, rippling pleasure as he moved to possess her, and she drew him down to her, grasping his hips, crying his name.

She was conscious only of his eyes now. Soft black velvet with a blue sheen, gazing into hers with an intensity she thought she had forgotten forever.

'Jake,' she whispered tremblingly.

His fingers fleetingly brushed her face in mute reply and then he was carrying her inexorably to the very edge of delight, his whole body telling her that he would carry her over it, too, until her senses spiralled away into a kaleidoscope of ecstasy.

Her whole consciousness seemed to splinter. Only one constant remained. Jake.

The room was dark when she woke and she stretched languorously, feeling Jake's body heat against hers, knowing that when he awoke she would be able to ex-

plain everything to him, to make him see how wrong he
was about her.

Reaching out for her rucksack, she pulled at a shirt,
but as she switched on the bedside light, she could see
it was not hers, but Jake's. Her fingers felt the stiffness
of a card in the front pocket and she realized that it was
Jamie's picture—the one Jake had found in her flat so
long ago it now seemed.

Her fingers shaking, she pulled out the photo and
studied it in the soft pool of light. No wonder Jake was
in such high demand as a photographer, she thought.
He had encapsulated Jamie's character exactly in the
fraction of a second that it took for his camera's shutter
to open and close.

There were times when she had looked at Jamie in the
flesh and wondered if he had been moulded from gold.
Jake had dark hair, a lean dark face and eyes that looked
far into the distance—until he smiled. Then his expression could light a whole roomful of people, and they
would stay lit even after he left.

Jamie, by contrast, lit up faces wherever he went, but
left no feeling of warmth behind him.

Sara's forefinger traced the outline of the bold, con-
fident smile, the wide blue eyes that, no matter how much
you shouted for attention, never quite seemed to register
your presence, and she sighed.

She turned to Jake, but his eyes, soft in the dim light,
hardened as his glance fell from her face to the photo.
'Sighing won't bring him back,' he remarked coldly,
whisking the picture from her hand.

'I wasn't...' began Sara, reaching out to him and then
stopping, shaken by the sudden contemptuous look on
his face.

'Don't insult me with some explanation you've made
up on the spur of the moment,' grated Jake. 'You just

never change, do you? I never thought I'd be caught out twice, Sara, but you...' He shook his head. 'What a fool I've been. I thought I was immune to you and you've played me as easily as you did Jamie.'

'No, Jake, please...' Sara pleaded.

He made a little impatient gesture with his hand. 'It's too late, Sara. Far too late. The gravy train stopped for you the night Jamie died. There's no getting back on it.'

She swallowed hard. 'I keep telling you,' she said desperately, 'it wasn't like that.'

He shook his head. 'Of course not,' he agreed wearily. 'It's just not true that Jamie bought you expensive things and lent you enormous amounts, which you never repaid despite the fact that you also got an allowance,' he said with cold sarcasm. 'I guess, for his sake, I should be touched that you at least seem to miss him.'

'You've got it all wrong, Jake,' she persisted.

'Have I?' he said. 'What about that letter I found in your handbag?'

'It isn't what you think,' she forced out.

'On the contrary,' he countered. 'It summed up all my worst imaginings.'

She stared at him, frustrated to the point of recklessness in how she was going to get him to believe her. 'You two were so different,' she burst out at last. 'But if there is one thing you had in common, it has to be sheer pigheadedness.'

Jake shrugged. 'Black sheep and golden boy,' he remarked. 'That about sums us up, wouldn't you say?'

Sara looked at his face, closed where only a few minutes before it had been open. 'Fool's gold,' she whispered.

'Because there wasn't as much as you expected?' he inquired brutally. 'You must have gone through your own trust fund at the rate of knots. Tell me, what exactly did you spend it all on?'

Sara's throat suddenly constricted, tears beginning to well in her eyes. She rubbed them away hurriedly and swallowed. 'It doesn't matter,' she mumbled. 'Believe what you like. I'm sorry, Jake.'

'For yourself, or Jamie?' he asked coldly.

'For all of us,' she said quietly.

He opened his mouth to reply, but whatever he had been going to say was lost in the sound of a muffled boom. All the lights went out as the building shook to its very foundations.

Crossing quickly to the window, Jake looked out, his body outlined by the moon's cold silver. Stealing across to join him, Sara looked up at the grim lines of his face. 'What is it?' she breathed. 'What's happened?'

He pointed to an orange glow in the sky. 'A bomb, I think,' he replied. 'Must have been a pretty big one, too, to make this building shake all the way out here. Must be a good two miles.'

He turned to her. 'Better get dressed,' he said brusquely. 'God knows what's going to happen now.'

'Wouldn't it be better to pretend ignorance?' Sara said unsteadily. 'Then if anyone comes and finds us in bed, it'll be obvious we had nothing to do with it.'

He stared at her for a few moments. 'The time for playing games is over now, don't you think?' he said calmly. 'If anyone was to come for us in the next few minutes, where would you rather be? Fully dressed and alert, or in bed? Even you wouldn't like to put your clothes on in front of a gang of soldiers.'

Numbly she looked at him, the pit of her stomach sick with fear, then whirled about and ran to her rucksack. Selecting clothes by feel alone in the cool darkness, she pulled on a shirt and jersey.

Her jeans were still lying on the floor where Jake had thrown them while they made love—eons ago it now seemed—and she almost fell over in her hurry to drag them on.

'Here.' She looked up at the sound of Jake's voice and saw he was holding out his arm. 'Come on, quickly,' he said. 'Lean on me.'

'What for?' she retorted. 'So you can let me fall over?'

His jaw clenched. 'Don't mess about, Sara. I just know that when I started in this game, it was always the one skill I found difficult to master, putting my clothes on quickly in the dark.'

'What game was that?' she demanded bitterly, taking hold of his arm anyway and stumbling about on one leg as she pulled on a sock. 'You mean when some unsuspecting husband returned home too early, while you were no doubt upstairs with his wife?' she inquired acidly.

She couldn't see his eyes in the dark but the tone of his voice turned silky smooth. Always a danger sign with Jake. 'Of course,' he agreed suavely. 'But since you're the expert on cheating on people, I'm amazed you haven't already dived into the wardrobe out of some sort of reflex reaction.'

'I'd like to lock you in the wardrobe,' snarled Sara, sitting down to lace up her boots. 'And throw away the key.'

She stuffed the rest of her clothes, what she could find of them in the silvered darkness of the room, into her rucksack and pulled the draw-string tight. Jake, dressed, if she had to guess, in about five seconds flat, had gone back to the window.

'There doesn't seem to be any movement outside,' he said quietly.

'Perhaps everyone's forgotten us,' she replied hopefully.

'Perhaps,' he said with complete lack of conviction.

Suddenly thinking of something he had said earlier, she scurried to the bedside table and then back to Jake.

'Here,' she whispered hoarsely. 'If anybody does come, at least we've got a weapon.'

He looked down at what she was holding in her hand and his grim features relaxed minutely as he took hold of what she offered. It was the champagne bottle.

Jake gazed at her through the gloom, his fingers grasping the neck of the bottle lightly but surely. 'Maybe it would have been better if you had emptied it first,' he remarked deadpan.

She shrugged, trying hard to control the leaping fear within her. 'Oh, well,' she said as offhandedly as she could, 'if our man from the Government Tourist Agency arrives to check up on us, you get two chances now, don't you? If the bottle doesn't get him, maybe the alcohol will.'

He put the bottle down on the floor and looked once more out of the window.

'What's happening?' she demanded.

'Nothing,' he replied. 'That's what's so eerie. There's just that glow in the sky. We're too far away to hear—' He stopped, listening intently.

'What is it?' hissed Sara.

'A vehicle of some sort,' he said quietly. 'Coming fast.'

She could hear it now. And there was no mistaking the squeal of brakes as it came to a stop outside the hotel. She found herself clutching Jake's arm, needing the feeling of security that his warmth and strength gave her.

He looked down at her, half of his face lit by the moon, the other half in total darkness. 'You're such a bundle of contradictions, Sara,' he said at last, wonderingly. 'You're every rotten word in the dictionary, and yet in a tight spot, you're one of the bravest people I've ever seen.'

She withdrew her hand from his arm and looked up at him. 'I'm not a bad person, Jake,' she said seriously. 'Really I'm not. All this stuff with Jamie…' She shrugged helplessly, and his eyes darkened at her apparent flippancy. 'If we don't get out of this,' she began again, 'you have to believe, to know—'

'Of course we'll get out of this,' he replied brusquely.

She shook her head. 'You don't like me,' she whispered. 'So why try to comfort me when we both know that there might not be much time left?'

He stared at her through the gloom and shook his head almost in disbelief. 'This was too dangerous a game to play with you, Sara. I shouldn't have brought you here.'

'Dangerous or not, I'm glad you did,' she said softly, decisively. 'I've been running for nearly eight years. It was time to stop, no matter what else happens. I'm glad we're here together, even if you do still think the worst of me. It's better facing up to you than spending my life wondering where you are and what you're thinking.'

His hand reached for her and then dropped as if he'd thought better of it. He sighed heavily. 'We should never have made love,' he said roughly. 'After what happened all those years ago, it must be the second stupidest thing I've ever done.'

Sara stepped back as though he had slapped her in the face. Everything suddenly seemed to have stopped—time, the tiniest sounds, her heart. Even the darkness appeared to be waiting tensely for whatever was going to happen next.

He stared silently at her eyes, huge in the moonlight, and made an impatient gesture with his hands. 'I brought you out here because of Jamie. I wanted to find out exactly how you used him, and I wound up being trapped by your charms in just the same way as he did.'

'I made love with you because I love you,' she returned. 'I think I always have.'

He laughed harshly, the sound echoing round the room. 'You don't love me,' he grated. 'What we did happened simply because we were two people thrown together in an exceptionally tense situation.'

'So...so this happens to you every time you go on an assignment?' she said as boldly as she could, her body beginning to tremble uncontrollably.

'Not all jobs are as tense as this one,' he said, the mocking light in his eyes only too obvious. 'But it's been known to happen.'

'You—' she bit out before choking to a stop. 'I can't even begin to say what I think of you, Jake,' she whispered at last. 'You're so cruel. So hard. You keep thinking all the time about how wrongly other people behave, while you just ride roughshod all over them. I thought I could make you see the truth. But you won't listen. You don't want to listen. You just want to hurt me and go on hurting me for all the imagined wrongs I've done to you and your family. Even if you ground me into dust, you'd go on rubbing me into the floor.' She shook her head. 'I never knew anyone could hate so much.'

She could see his jaw tense, a muscle thudding in his cheek. 'I can't deny that you're an extremely attractive woman, Sara,' he grated. 'But I'd be a fool if I turned my back on the things I've learned about you.'

Sara could feel her throat tightening, the tears welling in her eyes. There was no other person in the world that she wanted to be close to—and yet it was as impossible as reaching out to another planet.

A furious rattling at the door broke the spell between them, and Jake crossed the room quickly. 'Stand over there,' he ordered. 'If only one or two come in, grab their attention and I'll do my best to take them out.'

'But, Jake, you can't—' she remonstrated.

'Just do it,' he broke in, hefting the champagne bottle. 'We have no choice.'

CHAPTER EIGHT

THE doorknob turned and Sara licked dry lips. How on earth was she going to face a mob of soldiers? But as the door opened, the only person she could see was the boy monk they had met the day before, standing with impassive dignity in the gloom.

Weak with relief, Sara ran to him and drew him into the room like an old friend. 'What's going on?' she panted as Jake looked out into the corridor and then closed the door. 'Please tell us.'

'Everybody has gone from here,' the boy said. 'There have been bombs everywhere tonight. Including the airport. Lama Banideya sent me. You must get away over the mountains to Nepal.'

'In the Jeep?' asked Jake.

The boy nodded. 'There is a full tank and spare cans. I took them from the soldiers' barracks.'

'Won't they miss them?' breathed Sara.

'No,' replied the boy. 'There is too much chaos. You must get away now, or it will be too late.'

Not daring to believe their luck, they stole down the stairs and outside. The boy stood watching, his robes ruffling gently in the wind, as Jake started the Jeep.

'There's just one thing,' asked Sara. 'How did you get the key to our room?'

The boy beamed at her. 'It was on the board at reception. I tried all of them in turn.' He turned to Jake. 'The lama remembered you from before. We have been watching out for you since you left the other hotel.' He held out a small object. 'Good luck,' he said solemnly. 'Tell the world what you have seen.'

Jake took the small package and reached out to squeeze the boy's shoulder. 'Come with us,' he urged. But the boy shook his head. 'No. I have duties to my country. I must stay here.'

Jake looked at him for a long moment and then nodded slowly. Turning the steering wheel, he put his foot down, and the Jeep began to power away.

Sara, twisting round in her seat, looked back at the small, lonely figure for as long as she could before it was swallowed up by the darkness. She turned to Jake with a sigh. 'Do you think he'll be all right?'

He shrugged. 'I hope so. The monks will take care of him.'

She swallowed hard. 'What about us?' she asked as matter-of-factly as she could.

He glanced at her and sighed. 'Realistically?' She nodded. He changed gear. 'We have a good chance,' he said finally. 'But after the past few days, I don't like to take anything for granted. I came this route before, when I was here two years ago.'

'Think you can remember it?' she asked anxiously and was rewarded by a grim smile.

'Let's hope so. But if we get lost, I hear the scenery can be stunning.'

She stared at the road ahead, silence enveloping them.

Strong fingers cupped her chin and turned her face to his. 'Not even the slightest word of complaint or regret about getting you into this situation?' he inquired, his light words belying the dark seriousness of his eyes, flickering from her to the road.

She looked at him for a long moment, schooling herself to calm the unsteady beat of her pulse at his touch. 'I promised myself I'd never speak to you again after what happened this evening,' she said at last, pulling his fingers away.

'Is that something you're going to keep up all the way to Nepal?' he asked.

She shook her head. 'No,' she replied. 'I'm just tired, I suppose. It's as though I can't take in everything that's going on. I want to hate you, but you seem to have the monopoly on that emotion. I just feel numb.'

'If we get out of here alive,' he remarked, 'you can hate me as much as you like.'

She glared at him, anger suddenly surging through her at the completely false picture he had created of her. 'Don't think I won't, Jake. You think you can charm any woman you meet with those soft, dark eyes of yours and that stupid dimple that only shows when you smile in a certain way, but I'm over you forever.'

'Obviously,' he replied softly.

Furious, she opened her mouth to tell him exactly what she thought of him, but he got in first.

'Forget it, Sara. I wound you up and I'm sorry. If we make Kathmandu in one piece, I tell you, I'll be so glad I'll even stand still while you slap my face.

'But right now we have to rely on each other. There are plenty of people out there—' he waved his hand in front of them '—who'll be sniping at us for real. Let's not you and I do the job for them.'

She turned away and looked down at the road hurtling under the Jeep. Why did he have to be so right? To make her feel so childish? She bit her lip and straightened in her seat. No one was going to be able to accuse her of not rising to the occasion. If he wanted a truce, he'd get one. But one way or another, it was definitely going to be extremely temporary.

'I meant to ask you,' she said after a while. 'What was it that the boy gave you?'

Jake glanced at her and then turned his attention once more to the rising, rocky route in front of them. 'My miniature camera,' he said.

The road was too rugged to allow Sara any real sleep, but nevertheless she kept dozing off and then being jerked awake again as the Jeep bounced over the rock-strewn track.

And it was so cold. Clinging on for dear life, she dug about in her rucksack and pulled out the pair of nylon over-trousers she had so despised when Jake had bought them for her.

'I hate to say this,' she said after managing to shimmy into them and collecting three bruises in the process. 'But I'm glad you made me take this outfit. You can say I told you so if you like, and I'll try not to flinch too much if you want to crow.'

He glanced at her, and her mouth dropped open as he actually smiled. 'Wish I could stop to take a picture. The news room will never believe me when I tell them I've seen you wearing lime green nylon and no make-up.'

'You're right,' she bit out, completely floored by his friendly tones. 'No one will believe you.'

'Back in London you were always so perfectly turned out,' he mused. 'As if you'd just stepped out of a bandbox. Hair, make-up, clothes. I'm beginning to think you used your vanity as some kind of protective armour.'

'You need something to protect you in this job,' Sara replied seriously. 'There are plenty of people waiting to take pot-shots at you, without handing them a reason on a plate like your appearance not being up to scratch.'

'And you were such a scruffy little girl,' he reminded her. 'It was one of the things I liked about you.'

Why did even the simplest conversations with him have to end with her feeling as though her heart were being squeezed in two?

'What if I went and jumped in a puddle now?' she demanded caustically. 'Would it make you feel any better towards me?'

'If you went to jump in a puddle now,' said Jake, zigzagging expertly round a fallen boulder that had loomed up in the Jeep's headlights, 'I'd leave you behind.'

'Just what I'd expect from you,' she snarled. 'And don't think I wouldn't do the same thing.'

He smiled to himself. 'You got any of those tissues left?' he inquired. 'Out of that seemingly inexhaustible supply you had in that handbag of yours?'

'Why?' she demanded sarcastically. 'Do you want me to dab your fevered brow or something?'

'No,' he replied gently. 'I was just thinking of waving a white flag.'

'Don't take the mickey out of me,' she snapped. 'You're the one who's making me feel like this. You've played with my emotions, used me and now you're laughing at me.'

'I'm not laughing at you,' he said, looking straight ahead. Then glancing at her quickly, he shrugged. 'I'm sorry, Sara. I've played this all wrong. I shouldn't have brought you out here.'

Sara stared at the road in front. 'But you still blame me for Jamie's death, don't you?' she said softly. 'You still hate me.'

'I don't know what to think any more,' he said wearily. 'You never give any explanations, except to claim over and over again that you are absolutely innocent. But from all the other evidence, what you say isn't particularly convincing.'

She felt her heart fall at his cool tones. 'When I wanted to tell you,' she declared, 'you'd already made up your mind to believe the worst.'

'Why should I listen when I knew that anything you were going to tell me was going to be a heap of lies?' he countered.

She breathed in deeply and looked away. She would never win this argument. Would never convince him. There was absolutely no use reasoning with him.

The headlights speared a path through the darkness, which seemed to be turning a soft grey. If Sara looked to the side, she was certain she could see vague shapes.

'Dawn's coming,' she said laconically, yawning so much she thought her face was going to split in two.

Jake passed a weary hand through his thick, dark hair and down over his chin. 'I need a shave,' he said wearily. 'I don't know why they call it designer stubble. It certainly doesn't grow to order.'

'Let me drive,' suggested Sara, so suddenly that she surprised herself as much as Jake. 'Go on,' she encouraged him, fired by the idea of doing something at last. 'We won't get anywhere fast if you fall asleep at the wheel. I'll just follow the track and wake you at the first sign of any trouble.'

As if in answer, he pulled to a halt and got out and stretched. 'OK,' he agreed. 'Makes sense. But this is not the same as scorching down the Kings Road with a traffic policeman after you, so go carefully.'

Jake, much to her annoyance, managed to sleep like a baby for the next three hours. How could he just drop off so easily when she had only been able to doze in ten-minute snatches? Infuriating man. The scenery was stunning as they shot through it, and she shocked herself with the sudden notion that she would like to share it with him.

But the idea of his reaction at being woken to look at a particularly beautiful line of mountains was not to be thought of. Every so often she glanced in her rear-view mirror, fearful of what she might see following them. But there was nothing.

She stopped finally to refill the tank from the big jerrycan strapped to the back, but as she leaned over to get it, Jake's hand closed over hers. 'I'll take the can,' he said. 'It's too heavy for you.'

He was so close to her she could feel his body heat, and her heart gave a double thump. Why did he have to affect her like this? 'I can manage,' she protested, trembling at the contact.

'With all those emotions you're carrying round,' he said softly, 'I'm surprised you can manage the jerrycan, too.'

'Don't make fun of me,' she said tightly.

'I'm sorry,' he whispered, his lips coming down on hers. It felt so right to be kissed like this, she found herself thinking. It would be so easy to give in to the gentle pressure of his mouth, to relax and take the comfort he was offering. So right and so wrong.

She put her hands on his chest and pushed. 'Don't do this,' she cried out. 'It means nothing to you. How can you, when you hate me so much?' He stroked her cheek with his fingers and she trembled violently. 'And,' she grated, 'when I hate you?'

His hand dropped, but he was still too close. He sighed deeply. 'I'll refill the tank,' he said after a moment. 'Get back in the passenger seat and have a rest. You've done brilliantly.'

She looked up into his lean brown face and, taken completely by surprise at his praise, began to blush furiously. Turning sharply, she stumbled away, sudden tears streaming down her cheeks.

She half expected him to stop her, to take her in his arms once more and kiss her, but he didn't move, only his blue-black eyes following her as she got back into the Jeep, her heart going nineteen to the dozen.

How dare he affect her like that even when he had told her how little he cared for her? How dare he say he was sorry like that when he obviously didn't mean a word he said? Sorry indeed. Damn him.

She scrubbed her face hurriedly with her knuckles and looked at her face in the rear-view mirror. Red-rimmed eyes and blotched cheeks stared back.

There was no way she was going to let him see she had been crying. She blinked briskly and swallowed. A few minutes that seemed like an eternity passed, and then Jake swung himself back into the driving seat. 'Not far now,' he said as if nothing had happened. 'The border with Nepal is only a few miles away, but it may prove the trickiest part.'

'I don't care,' Sara replied defiantly. 'I'm so hungry I feel like I'd brave anything to get somewhere where there's food.'

'They have shops devoted to nothing but puddings in Kathmandu,' Jake told her. 'You could spend an entire day there eating nothing but lemon meringue pie, if you wanted.'

'Don't talk to me about puddings,' she replied feelingly. 'If I get out of this in one piece I'll never go on a diet again. Ever.'

'There's some walnuts in my rucksack...' Jake began, and then glancing sideways at her as she shook her head violently, added, 'They're perfectly all right, you know.'

'Actually,' she admitted after a few moments, 'I've already eaten them.'

*   *   *

Soon they were cresting yet another ridge, but this time from the top she could see the little checkpoint in the valley. Soldiers, like ants, clustered round it. 'There are troops all over the place,' she muttered.

Jake nodded. 'The border's probably been closed since the bombs last night,' he said thoughtfully. 'Nobody will do anything until we get right up close. This is a government Jeep, so they'll probably think it contains officials of some sort.'

'But it's hopeless,' she breathed. 'We're never going to make it through that lot.'

Jake glanced at her. 'Want to go back?' he said grimly.

She met his eyes. 'No,' she grated.

The checkpoint was drawing closer and closer. Soon it would be obvious to the most short-sighted soldier on guard duty that the Jeep was not carrying government officials.

Sara had a terrible desire to throw herself out of the Jeep and just run. Anywhere. She clutched hold of her seat tightly and fought to breathe calmly, too terrified not to look exactly where they were hurtling.

She swallowed. 'I'm sure they're going to shoot at us. What...what will we do?'

Jake changed gear and put his foot flat on the floor. 'Pray,' he said grimly.

The soldiers were running now, pointing guns at them and shouting. Sara closed her eyes and then opened them again to see the guards scattering as the Jeep drove straight at them and smashed through the barrier.

'We did it!' she yelled, throwing her arms around Jake as the Jeep careered away from the wrecked border post, then kissing him on the cheek. 'We did it!'

Jake looked in his rear-view mirror and kept on driving. 'Nearly,' he corrected her, grinning broadly as he kept the Jeep rattling along. 'We're only in no man's land. All we have to do now is convince the Nepalese border guards to let us through without our passports.'

'Well, just don't run over any of them,' Sara replied euphorically.

The little Nepalese border post soon came into view and Jake slowed and then stopped by the barrier. There were far more soldiers here than at the Bandhul check-point, Sara noticed. Too many to drive through even if they had dared. They had obviously heard of the troubles and were on full alert.

She stared at one young soldier as he hefted his gun, but her thoughts were interrupted by a man in a different uniform bustling out of the little shack by the barrier.

He held out his hand. 'Passports, visas.'

Jake got out of the Jeep. 'We need to talk to you about that,' he said. 'I'm afraid...'

But the official was no longer paying any attention to Jake. He stood staring at Sara until she looked away in embarrassment. But when she looked back at him, he was still staring. 'What's the matter?' she asked frostily. 'Have I got a spot on my nose or something?' she glanced at Jake's darkening expression and, remembering with awful clarity the hole they were in, mumbled, 'Sorry.'

'No, no,' said the official, who was staring at her so closely he had obviously not heard a word she'd said. 'What is your name?'

'Sara Thornton.'

'*The* Sara Thornton?' he breathed.

She glanced at Jake, who shrugged and nodded. He apparently didn't care what she said so long as they got through this.

'I—I'm not sure,' she stammered. 'I...'

But the official had whisked back into his shed and come out again, clutching a glossy magazine, which he thrust in front of Sara's nose. 'Look,' he said. 'Your picture. You wrote about our king when he was in London. I am reading it just now. It is a beautiful article. Beautiful picture—'

'Thank you,' began Sara, not certain whether to laugh or cry at Jake's expression. 'That's so sweet of you. You don't know how glad I am you enjoyed reading it.'

'Not at all,' he replied affably. 'Not at all. What can I do for you?'

'The people in Bandhul took our passports,' said Jake. 'We'd like you to allow us into your country.'

'Of course I will let you in.' The official beamed at Sara. 'You have met the king.' He looked doubtfully at Jake. 'That looks like a very dangerous man,' he said in a hoarse stage whisper. 'Will you vouch for him?'

'Oh, I think so,' said Sara, trying hard, without much success, to keep a straight face. 'He doesn't look half so fierce when he's had a shave.'

Silence lengthened between them as Jake drove on towards Kathmandu. 'If you don't stop beaming soon,' he observed mildly, 'your face will stay like that forever.'

'I can't help it,' she replied simply. 'I keep thinking of your face when we were at that border post.'

'I never realized you were so famous,' he remarked deadpan. 'Fancy—I'm sitting next to *the* Sara Thornton. I must remember to ask you for your autograph sometime.'

'You can have it,' she said happily. 'On my next expenses claim form. And be warned. It'll be a whopper.'

She looked at the grim lines on his face, her happiness faltering. 'I must say, for a man who just got out of near civil war by the skin of his teeth, you don't look very happy.'

He sighed. 'No, I don't suppose I do,' he said at last. 'I guess because I just realized that this was my last assignment. When I go back to London, it'll be to sit behind a desk and watch other people go off round the world.'

'Yes,' agreed Sara, unable at that moment to feel unhappy about anything. 'But think of all the power and glory, and pots and pots of money you'll make.'

'Is that really what it takes to keep you happy?' inquired Jake. 'Pots of money?'

'Well, maybe not pots,' she replied, blissfully unaware of the iciness creeping into his voice. 'But a few jam jars of it always come in handy.'

'So all those bank statements I saw of Jamie's were quite correct after all, then?' he probed. 'And that's why you stuck with him until, of course, Pa cut off both your allowances?'

'That's an outrageous thing to say,' she gasped, realizing with a sudden cold feeling how neatly he had trapped her. 'I stuck with Jamie because he was my brother. We weren't attracted to each other. And I certainly didn't drop him because of the money.'

'Why, then?' he pressed her.

She glanced at him and then away again. 'It doesn't matter,' she said. 'As you've already told me, you just believe what you want to.' She lifted her chin and turned to him. 'But I've never relied on other people's money. I've always paid my own way.'

'That's one way of putting it when you're always up to your neck in debt,' observed Jake.

They were in Kathmandu proper now and the Jeep screeched to a halt outside the biggest and best hotel.

'Here we are,' Jake grated. 'Guaranteed no yaks on the ground floor. Is it good enough for you?'

She stared at him, almost speechless with hurt. 'Why are you being so rotten?' she whispered. 'Now, of all times?' She swallowed. 'I just can't take any more, Jake,' she muttered. 'Please don't treat me this way.'

He rubbed his face with his hand and sighed. 'You're the person who said she hated me,' he said. 'You're the one who's lied and kept on lying about my brother.'

He looked straight into her eyes. 'Let's face it, Sara. All you want in life is enough money to keep you in a style you'd like to become accustomed to.'

'That's unfair!' she burst out, not caring that several people on the pavement had stopped and were staring at them. 'But then I might have expected it from you because that's all you ever are—unfair.'

He opened his mouth but she swept on. 'You dragged me out to Bandhul in the middle of a bloody great rebellion just because you thought you could make me give you every single detail about what Jamie and I said to each other before he died. Well, what makes you think you had a right to do that?'

'He was my brother,' Jake replied simply. 'And I thought you were hiding something that could be important about his death.'

He leaned towards her. 'Trouble is,' he said grimly, 'I've come to the conclusion that what you were hiding was your own shabby behaviour.'

With a sob, Sara stumbled out of the Jeep and grabbed her rucksack. 'Well, it may surprise you to know that I loved Jamie,' she yelled. 'Loved him like the brother he became. And I do hate you. Don't ever forget it!'

Jake stared at her coldly and then started up the Jeep. 'I don't care how you feel about me,' he snarled. 'I've saved your neck. Now get us some rooms and get on to

London and file your story,' he bit out. 'I'm going to get my pictures sent and see about some replacement passports.'

She stood on the pavement, tears streaming down her cheeks as the Jeep roared off.

The hotel receptionist looked sympathetically at her as she trailed into the lobby and up to the desk. 'Two rooms, please,' she mumbled.

'I am sorry, madam, he told her. 'We have only one single. The only other room available is the honeymoon suite.'

Her lips twisting at the irony of it all, Sara took the key for the single room and wearily plodded off upstairs.

In the end, ringing London and putting over a news story about the outbreak of rebellion in Bandhul seemed the easiest thing she had done in days. The connection was clear, and relating the straight facts, as far as she knew them, took her mind off everything but the job in hand.

But when she put the phone down again and looked round her hotel room, she wanted to roll into a ball and cry. She couldn't remember ever having felt so miserable before. She'd said she hated Jake, but it wasn't true. The trouble was he didn't want her love. All he wanted was to believe the worst about her.

Sara wandered listlessly into the bathroom and showered. She couldn't even take comfort in the fact that she'd carried out her job with any particular effectiveness. Heaven only knew how she was going to write the colour piece that Emma had wanted. All in all, she had been about as efficient in Bandhul as a chocolate teapot, she thought gloomily.

And she had been so dead set on keeping her word to Jamie that she had ended up making the one and only man she'd ever truly loved turn against her.

With their assignment over, Jake would be bound to disappear almost totally out of her life. She might see him in a corridor at work, but that would be it. She had managed to screw up enough courage once to tell him she loved him. And he had laughed in her face. She could not do it again.

She stared moodily at her jeans as she pulled them back on. They were filthy, but she had nothing else to wear. Thinking evil thoughts about arrogant men who threw entire suitcases full of good clothes into airport bins, she stumped downstairs in search of the bar. If ever someone needed a stiff drink, it was now.

Jake was already there, his unshaven face and mud-spattered jeans making him look, if anything, even more sexy.

Sara gritted her teeth and held her head up as she walked past him. After the way he had treated her outside, she had better choose a seat as far away as possible from him. But to her utter shock, he put out a hand and gripped her wrist.

'Sara,' he said huskily.

She trembled. 'That's me, all right,' she replied as lightly as she could.

He looked up at her steadily. 'I owe you an apology.' Her jaw dropped, and his lips quirked. 'There's no need to look quite so shocked,' he drawled. 'I've behaved pretty appallingly towards you over the past few days.'

She swallowed. 'I haven't exactly been the model of good behaviour myself.'

He smiled up into her eyes. 'True,' he said, nodding.

She wrenched her hand away. 'Why, you arrogant—'

The amusement in his gaze was only too plain now. But he held up his hands in mock surrender. 'Go on,' he told her. 'Insult me. I can take it.'

She lifted her chin. 'I don't want to expend the effort.'

He stood up slowly and she stepped back. 'Why don't you sit down?' he said quietly. 'I'll get us both a drink.'

'I want something strong and lots of it,' she told him.

'What you want and what you need are two entirely different things,' he replied grimly.

Her drink when it came was a tall one, so cold her fingers left trails on the cloudy glass, with a big slice of lemon bumping in among the ice cubes. 'I've been looking for something like this ever since we got to Bandhul.' She smiled involuntarily, thinking of how she had barged into the hotel's yak population.

'It's only mineral water,' he said, shrugging. 'Considering the effect alcohol has on you when you haven't eaten, I thought it was best.'

She glanced at him, thinking of the afternoon before, and then looked quickly away. 'You're probably right,' she mumbled. 'I mean, neither of us wants another episode like yesterday evening.'

'Sara—' he began.

But she was too quick for him. He was probably going to come out with a lot of platitudes he didn't mean, and her pride couldn't bear it. 'I don't want any apologies or explanations,' she said, banging her glass down on the table. 'What's happened, happened. Leave it at that.'

Looking up, she saw his face harden. 'If you like,' he said tersely. He stood up and held out a hand to her. 'Come on. I guess we could both do with something to eat.'

Sara bit her lip. It was torture, being this close to him and knowing that he was merely being polite to her. She didn't know if she could stand the unbearable intimacy of being in a restaurant with him.

'I...I'm not hungry,' she muttered uncertainly.

'Don't be ridiculous,' he rasped. 'You haven't had anything proper to eat since I don't know when.'

She glared at him. 'Don't bully me,' she said haughtily.

His eyes narrowed. 'You've had a handful of nuts and a pot of yoghurt in the past twenty-four hours. That's not even enough to feed your ego on.'

'So?' she said with a bravado she didn't feel. 'I might be on a diet for all you know.'

A glimmer of amusement warmed his eyes. 'I thought you said you'd never go on one again,' he said innocently. And then before she could make any retort, he added, 'In any case, the last time you announced to the office you were on a diet, I saw you in a restaurant the next day, munching happily through three courses. And when the loud-mouthed poseur you were with pushed his pudding to one side, you ate that, too.'

Her jaw dropped. 'You've been spying on me.'

'Of course,' he drawled. 'I have so little else to occupy my time, I spend my entire life dressed in a dirty mac trailing you the length and breadth of Kensington High Street.' He leaned towards her. 'Now, are you coming to dinner under your own steam, or am I going to carry you there and force-feed you chocolate mousse?'

'Chocolate m-mousse?' she quavered, his eyes not two inches from her own. He nodded, and she suppressed the longing to touch his face.

'Do I take that soft look in your eyes to mean yes?' he inquired.

She stood up suddenly. This man was absolutely impossible. 'I'm...I'm...' she said wildly.

He put a hand under her elbow and guided her expertly from the bar. 'Good,' he said firmly. 'I'm glad that's settled.'

CHAPTER NINE

IF ONLY the tragedy surrounding Jamie hadn't occurred, Sara thought as she pushed her dinner around on her plate, then it would have been easy to enjoy this evening. But then, she reflected glumly, she probably wouldn't have been here at all.

Jake said nothing to spook her, but she began wondering if he would bring up the subject of Jamie again— or almost worse, continue in his belief that whatever she had to say wasn't worth hearing. She let the waiter take away her almost-untouched plate and then as coffee was placed in front of her she wondered if the assault was about to begin.

But before either of them could say anything, the shrill cut-glass tones of a voice she knew so well sliced right across their thoughts like nails being dragged down a blackboard.

'How marvellous. I've found you at last.' Standing by Jake, staring fondly down at him, was Emma. 'Mind if I join you?' She smiled vaguely at Sara and, not waiting for an answer, pulled up a chair.

'What are you doing here?' gasped Sara, unable to take her eyes from her boss, immaculately dressed as ever.

Emma looked astonished that she should even ask. 'We were worried about you,' she said, looking at Jake. 'You wouldn't believe what started happening in London when you disappeared and the rebellion started in Bandhul. Your father—'

'Is he all right?' demanded Jake.

'Fine,' replied Emma. 'He's fine. Between you and me, I think he rather enjoyed all the hoo-ha. Ringing the Foreign Office and chewing them out because they couldn't bring pressure to bear on some tinpot dictatorship.'

Sara bit her lip. 'I hope he's all right,' she said doubtfully. 'The last time I saw him, he didn't look very well at all.'

Jake glanced at her. 'When did you see him?' he demanded.

Sara was suddenly confused. 'I went to see him in hospital,' she mumbled. 'But I don't think he was in a fit state to recognize me, really.'

'When was this?' pressed Jake.

'While you were away on assignment,' Sara reluctantly admitted.

Jake's eyes softened fractionally. 'I thought you hadn't bothered to see him at all.'

Emma laid a hand on his arm. 'Darling,' she remonstrated, 'stop cross-examining her about hospitals and dates and things. The poor girl looks all in.'

Sara withdrew hands from her coffee-cup and hid them in her lap. She was suddenly horribly conscious of how beautifully casual Emma looked. As though she had been flown over in a plastic case like some exotic orchid. She looked down at her own bitten nails and travel-stained clothes and stood up abruptly. 'I'm tired,' she said brusquely. 'I think I'll go to bed.'

Emma fished in her handbag. 'Here. You'll need these at some point. Spare passport and ticket home. You might as well have them now.'

Sara took them. 'Thanks,' she said briefly. And then turning on her heel almost ran out of the room.

*   *   *

The receptionist was most helpful when she inquired about flight times. 'Your ticket is for tomorrow,' he told her. 'But I am sure you will have no trouble in exchanging it for an earlier flight. I believe there is one later tonight.'

'Get me on it,' pleaded Sara. Jake and Emma would no doubt be sharing the honeymoon suite tonight, she thought bitterly, and she knew that it was more than she could bear to stay under the same roof.

It was bad enough having to sit there listening to Emma coo at him over the coffee-cups. 'Darling' indeed, she thought disgustedly.

Jake had denied there was anything in their relationship. But why else should Emma fly all the way out here?

Sara tapped her fingers nervously on the counter. 'And get me a taxi, please.'

'There's one outside,' the receptionist began and then, as she hurried to the door, called after her, 'What about your luggage?'

She thought of Jake and the scuffle they had had over her suitcase at the airport. But then she thought of Emma and her mind hardened. 'Chuck it all in the bin,' she said decisively. 'I never want to see that rucksack again as long as I live.'

Her flat seemed very small when she returned, and her misery was sharpened when she opened the front door and found the small mountain of suitcases she had packed for the trip. If everything she saw in the flat reminded her in some way of Jake, then going to the office was bound to be murder.

She simply couldn't do it. Even the idea of seeing Jake and Emma together—and her imagination was working with sickening clarity—was like rubbing salt in a wound.

The worst of it was that Jake had said there was nothing in the relationship. How could he have lied to her like that, while accusing her of not telling the truth? She sighed.

But if she was honest with herself, that wasn't the worst of it at all. The worst was thinking of Jake with another woman.

She was so tired and strung out she knew she wouldn't sleep. Wearily she sat down and began working out her background piece to the news story.

Anything to stop her thinking about Jake. Determinedly she wrote on. She would need to file it soon. And then when she had done that she could start trying to forget everything that had happened and pick up her life again.

A tear splashed onto the last sentence and her biro refused to write through it. She bit her lip and threw down her pen. She was so tired. So desperately tired.

Unable to work, she stumbled to bed and lay down fearing that she would not be able to sleep. In seconds, she had dropped into oblivion.

The light showed greyly through her curtains when she finally awoke. Yawning, Sara shambled through her flat, clutching a cup of coffee and trying, without success, to work out how many hours it had been since she had caught that flight from Nepal. She thought of Jake and Emma and banged her coffee-cup on the table. Damn them both.

Picking up the copy she had written on Bandhul, she rang for a motorbike messenger and thought grimly about her return to the office.

But it was no good. She just couldn't face them. With trembling fingers, she rang up work to tell them she was going to be off sick indefinitely.

'What's the matter with you?' said one of her colleagues.

'I haven't the faintest idea,' Sara confided unthinkingly, adding hurriedly, 'I think it's a sort of debilitating allergy.'

She could hear muffled voices at the other end of the line and then Jake's voice, loud and clear, stung down the wires. 'The only allergy you've got,' he grated, 'is one to work. And it better clear up in the next few minutes because features needs your background piece on Bandhul. Like yesterday.'

'I haven't had a great deal of sleep,' she bit out, her heart hammering. 'And that flight I took seemed to stop everywhere in the world where there's an airport.'

'Your fault for disappearing in the middle of the night without a by-your-leave,' he snapped. 'Do you know how worried Emma and I were about you?'

'I can imagine,' she retorted. 'You must have lost a lot of sleep.'

'It's just as well for you we're separated by a telephone wire,' he said coldly.

'You don't scare me,' Sara forced out.

'Really?' he said with deceptive softness. 'So why aren't you in the office?'

She swallowed and lifted her chin. 'I'm tired and I don't feel well,' she quavered as bravely as she could.

'How would you like to spend six months reporting on an environmental mission to the Antarctic?' he inquired icily.

'You wouldn't,' she whispered, aghast. 'Anyway, I get seasick.'

'If you think I bust a gut getting those pictures in Bandhul just so everything could all be screwed up by some prima donna showbiz writer who's got a fit of the vapours,' Jake ground out, 'then you've got another think coming.'

'I've written the piece,' said Sara, wondering if she was ever going to be able to breathe properly again. 'A bike messenger is bringing it over.'

'You better come to the office in person, or you'll be on your bike,' snarled Jake. 'There's plenty of other work you can be doing in the meantime.'

'Don't you order me about,' she retorted fiercely. 'Who do you think you are?'

'Nobody much,' he grated. 'Just your boss, that's all.'

'I liked you better when you were just a photographer,' she spat. 'You weren't a particularly nice person, but at least you weren't power mad.'

'Do you know exactly how powerful I am?' he asked, his voice at once dangerously silky.

She swallowed. 'I don't care.'

There was the sound of tearing paper and her forehead wrinkled in confusion. What was he up to now? 'That was the sound of your expenses going down the Swanee,' he informed her a few moments later. 'And they were just for last month. Wait until I start in on the whoppers you put in for the month before.'

'You absolute beast,' she breathed. 'How dare you!'

'I'm power mad, remember?' he grated.

There was a short silence. 'I think you'll like the article,' she said in a small voice. On the other end of the line, the silence lengthened as she gabbled on. 'You were right to risk that trip in that rotten old taxi. My copy wouldn't have been half so good without all the eye-witness stuff about the troops on the streets and the aeroplanes and so forth.'

Desperately she waited for Jake to reply. Perhaps he had been distracted by Emma and simply forgotten she was there. But when he spoke again, he sounded suddenly very tired. 'Good,' he said. 'I'll look forward to reading it.'

She gripped the telephone more tightly. 'If you like,' she forced out, 'I can order up another bike and send round my resignation, too.'

Jake sighed. 'Let's keep your contribution to air pollution to a minimum, shall we?' he drawled at last. The phone clicked and Sara was left listening to the loneliness of humming wires.

She showered and then crawled back into bed. If she woke up in fifty years' time, it would be too soon.

The shrilling of the doorbell pierced her sleep and dreamily she waited for it to stop. But it didn't stop. It just kept on and on until she slowly woke up and then, pulling on her dressing gown, stumbled sleepily to the Entryphone.

'Who is it?' she said, yawning.

'It's me. Jake. Let me in.'

Suddenly she was wide awake. 'Go away.'

'Let me in, Sara—' his voice crackled angrily through the box '—or I'll climb up your drainpipe.'

'I'd like to see you try,' she snarled. There was silence, and then suddenly terrified that he might just carry out his threat, she yelled down the Entryphone, 'Jake?'

Yes?' he replied calmly.

'You—' she began.

'Why don't you let me in?' he suggested reasonably. 'And then you can insult me in the comfort of your own home.'

Muttering evilly under her breath, she pressed the button to free the lock on the front door of her block of flats and waited nervously for Jake to come up.

There wasn't time to dress, and as she caught sight of herself in the hall mirror she shuddered nervously. She should be looking sleek and self-confident for this encounter, not like something that had just crawled out of a swamp.

Her hair had been wet when she had gone to bed and now it looked as though several birds had nested in it, brought up their young and then had disappeared trying to find a way out.

The door buzzed and she yanked it open. Jake was standing in front of her with an expression she couldn't quite place.

'Have I got three heads or something?' he inquired.

'No,' she replied, frowning. 'It's just that I'm not used to seeing you in a suit. You look so... different.'

He always had an air of authority, thought Sara. Even in his jeans and a muddy shirt, the soldiers in Bandhul had backed off when he'd accused them of mistreating her. But now, in his dark, well-cut suit and white shirt, he looked exactly what he was about to become—an assured and rather dangerous-looking corporate raider.

'Seen enough?' Jake's quiet tones seared across her thoughts and she stood back to let him in.

'Sorry,' she mumbled.

And then as she raised her eyes to his, she swallowed rapidly. Why did he have to make her feel so nervy?

'Don't stare at me like that,' she said faintly.

'Why not?' he inquired. 'You look very nice.'

'Nice?' she echoed.

'Yes,' he replied. 'Sort of charmingly tousled.'

Her jaw dropped and she pulled her robe more tightly round her. 'Are you really Jake Armstrong, my boss?' she inquired, 'or some sort of insanely polite imposter?'

'Oh, I'm Jake Armstrong all right,' he replied, turning in the middle of her sitting room to face her. 'Jake Armstrong, the man who can't even see the truth until he's battered over the head with it. That's who I am.'

She rubbed the sleep out of her eyes and looked at him groggily. 'What's the matter?' she asked, her misery returning like a lead weight as she remembered everything that had happened. 'You found something else to accuse me of?'

He shook his head. 'No, except of making me feel like a complete fool.'

She gazed at him for a moment and then shook her head. 'I must be going deaf,' she said at last. 'I could have sworn you just admitted to feeling foolish.'

He looked at her grimly. 'I did. I also discovered I owe you something.' She pushed a hand through her hair and looked at him confusedly. 'A box of hankies?' she hazarded.

'An apology,' he said with a slight smile. 'And I can't blame you for not making things very easy for me.'

She shrugged. 'Sorry, it's a trick I learned from you.'

'Are you always this prickly when you wake up?' he inquired.

'I don't know,' she said slowly. 'I generally wake up on my own. Although I don't expect you to believe that.'

The seconds ticked by as they gazed at each other.

'Are you still cross with me?' she finally uttered.

'Cross?' he echoed. 'I'll say. When I found out the truth about Jamie and his bungled financial dealings half an hour ago, I wanted to wring your neck.'

She took a step backwards and felt like she was falling over a cliff. 'What...what exactly did you find out?' she stammered.

'Only that you spent all your money trying to bail him out from those business deals he so spectacularly screwed up.' He took a step towards her. 'Why didn't you tell me, Sara? I've had people investigating Jamie's affairs, and I got their report this afternoon. You could have saved yourself a lot of heartache, you know.'

She subsided with a thud on her sofa. 'Jamie didn't want anybody to know. He made me promise,' she said.

'Do you know all the conclusions I jumped to about you and him?' he demanded, sitting down next to her. 'Do you know what I thought of you?'

She nodded, not daring to look up. 'Yes,' she said softly.

Jake stared at her, his eyes the darkness of a midnight sky. 'Then for God's sake, why didn't you tell me?' he grated.

'Because Jamie didn't want you to know,' she answered. 'He only ever wanted you and your father to admire him, to realize that he was just as good a businessman as you both. He didn't want you to come back and take over, Jake. He wanted to be the boss. He wanted to be like you.'

Jake wearily rubbed a hand over his face. 'I thought it was drugs or gambling,' he said ruefully.

Sara nodded. 'I know. That's partly in the end why I thought I'd tell you everything, but by then you didn't want to listen.'

He shot her a glance. 'I behaved pretty badly, didn't I?'

She shrugged. 'You weren't exactly a saint,' she replied with a small smile. 'But in a way I brought it on myself. I should have been open with you from the first, except...' She faltered.

'Except you didn't trust me,' supplied Jake. 'And considering everything that has happened between us, I can't really blame you for that.'

He sighed. 'Everything pointed to your being in cahoots with him. Everything I accused you of... on the one hand I couldn't believe it, but there seemed no other alternative.'

'Jamie hero-worshipped you, you know,' she said softly. 'Yes, he was lazy and irresponsible, but that didn't stop him from wanting what you had, to be what you were.

'All his dreams centred on being like you. Of course you couldn't see it. How could you? You spent all your time on assignments, or when you finally made your peace with your father, being closeted with him and learning the business.'

'We should have involved Jamie more,' said Jake. 'It's easy to see now, I suppose. But neither of us thought he was particularly interested. He certainly never showed any desire to be involved.' His lips twisted. 'He was my brother, and the last thing I would have thought he possessed was ambition to succeed in business. He never talked to me about it. Used to walk out of the room when Pa and I started discussing the deals we made.'

Sara smiled wryly. 'He wasn't really that interested. And that was the tragedy of it all. He hated what he called all the boring details. He just saw in his mind's eye the "big splash". He wanted to surprise you. He used to imagine out loud exactly how your face would look when he revealed this fantastic deal he'd pulled off.'

She slid her fingers unthinkingly into Jake's. 'But it was all just too much for him. I guess the sharks in the city must have rubbed their hands together in glee when they saw him coming.'

'Don't you think I can't imagine that?' Jake said grimly. 'Why couldn't you tell me?'

She looked at him and bit her lip. 'Because I thought you'd run out on me all those years ago,' she said quietly. 'I didn't know how to trust you any more.'

Jake stood up and stalked to the mantelpiece. 'And Jamie was at the bottom of that, too,' he said harshly.

'I always knew he was weak, but I never realized quite the lengths he would go to to get something he wanted.'

'I don't know what you mean,' whispered Sara, not wanting to admit to herself something she had always suspected.

'Jamie loved you,' Jake replied quietly. 'Or maybe—' he shrugged, a bitter little smile on his face '—he didn't want you to love me. He never really grew up, did he? Always wanted to be the centre of attention.'

Sara swallowed. 'Yes,' she admitted reluctantly. 'I never thought about it like that, but I can see now that it was true. I expect that's why he decided to get involved with those financial deals. To end up in the spotlight.'

'Even if you'd sent me a letter,' offered Jake, 'I could have done something.'

She looked down at her lap. 'I guess at the time Jamie was going under, I just wasn't thinking straight,' she reflected. 'I somehow assumed you wouldn't take me seriously.'

Her voice faltered. 'I—didn't want to be hurt again, Jake. I wanted to ring you and at the same time I didn't dare. I imagined that you had grown cold and hard and I couldn't bear to find out whether that was true or not.'

She shrugged wearily. 'Besides, the only thing that kept Jamie going when it all turned sour was the hope that he could still turn it round. He would have gone completely off the rails if he thought that I'd told you that he just couldn't cope.'

She sighed and looked pleadingly at Jake's reflection in the mirror above the fireplace. 'I couldn't go to your father because that was about the time he had his heart attack and he was just too ill. And you were almost constantly in some war zone or other,' she added softly. 'Even if I hadn't been terrified of contacting you, I didn't see how I could burden you. In any case—' she swallowed '—I didn't know what to say.'

Jake looked down at her. 'Try now,' he said quietly.

She leaned back against the sofa cushions and fiddled with the tie of her robe. 'I suppose it's quite simple, really,' she said after a moment. 'Jamie decided he wanted to make some big financial splash. But he wanted to do it on his own. He didn't want to go to your father for advice because that would have destroyed the object of the whole thing.'

She dropped her belt and wrapped her arms round herself. 'So he borrowed money at an enormously high rate of interest to fund some Euro-bond deal. Don't ask me to explain all the ins and outs. It seemed mind-bogglingly complicated to me, but Jamie thought it was all going to be brilliant.

'He really seemed to get off on the secrecy of it all,' she said. 'It was like a big game. Until everything fell through and he needed loads of money. It turned out he'd borrowed the money from some really dodgy people who turned quite nasty when he couldn't repay.'

'Go on,' encouraged Jake.

'I lent him all I could,' she said, her eyes wide with remembered pain as she stared up at him. 'But of course it wasn't enough. Your father cut off my allowance and Jamie's. And then I started to get some very heavy phone calls because Jamie was using this place as his base.

'It was sort of a black joke that every time he cashed a cheque to fend them off, he'd write my name on the stub. A sort of code, if you like. I suppose it was the same with all the names of those Bond Street shops. He certainly never bought me anything fantastically expensive.'

She shook her head. 'The main trouble was that he got almost fanatically secretive about everything. It was

as though he was living in a little world of his own, and
he could pretend that he had been a success—pretend
that he could afford, from money he had made himself,
to splash on me and luxurious things.'

She shrugged. 'And then I just didn't have any more
money, and I told him he'd have to come clean. Told
him to talk to Pa and try to sort something out. After
all, he may be a fairly formidable character, but he's not
an ogre.'

Jake glanced at her and then sat down. 'I'll tell him
you said so,' he said with a tight smile.

Sara ran her fingers through her hair. 'I don't know
that he'd feel particularly complimented,' she said
seriously. 'But it's true. Even after my mother ran off,
Pa didn't let me down. He could have washed his hands
of me. After all, I was foisted on him at the age of five
when he married my mother. But he looked after me.
Made sure I got a good start in life, and I'll never forget
it.'

Jake gazed at her. 'Is that why you went to see him
in hospital?'

She pulled her robe more carefully over one knee. 'Of
course. I knew he was angry with me because of the way
Jamie was behaving. And I knew he blamed me to a
certain extent. But I couldn't not go. I owe him so much.'

'Except perhaps an explanation?' observed Jake.

She bit her lip. 'I didn't know what to do. I wanted
to tell him. To tell you. But Jamie was practically off
the rails by then, and I didn't want to do anything that
would tip him over the edge.

'When I told him I just didn't have any more money
and suggested he tell his father, he was furious. Accused
me of betraying him. I tried to explain I wanted the best
for him. For everyone. But he simply wouldn't listen.
That's what that letter was all about.'

'That's why he called you cold and insensitive,' murmured Jake.

She nodded sadly. 'He couldn't understand that I was unable to bail him out any more. And he was so out of touch he blamed me for everything. That's what hurt most of all,' she whispered. 'That's why we rowed so badly on that last night. He was like a different person. It was terrifying. I just couldn't reason with him. And then he roared off in a temper and that was that.'

A tear slid down her cheek. 'I don't know whether it was an accident or not that he went off that bridge. I suppose I never will. But he was a big part of the only real family I ever had. And I miss him.'

She rubbed the back of her hand across her eyes and then looked up, anywhere except at Jake. 'Think I've got hay fever,' she said shakily, suddenly standing up, uncertain of herself and the man watching her so closely.

Jake took hold of her hand and pulled her down beside him. 'Why don't you let it all out, Sara,' he said softly. 'Cry.'

She shook her head wordlessly and gave him a watery smile. 'Too late for tears,' she choked out as lightly as she could. She scrabbled in a pocket for a handkerchief and blew her nose fiercely. 'The only thing Jamie had left, even when everything was crashing down around his ears, was his pride. I tried to make him see he had to swallow it. To admit his mistake and to get help. But even after he died, I couldn't bring myself to take that pride away from him.'

Jake's arm slid around her, more comforting than any words. 'You loved him more than any of us,' he said.

'I grew up with you both,' sniffed Sara. 'But after you left, he was all I had to remind me of you. He was the kid brother I'd always wanted. And I felt I had to take care of him, for your sake if nothing else.'

Jake pulled her close and reached into his shirt pocket. 'Here,' he said softly, handing her Jamie's photograph. 'You better have this.'

As her fingers curled around the little square card that she and Jake had rowed so spectacularly over, she pressed her head against his shoulder and sobbed until she thought her heart would break.

Jake held her close until her sobs subsided and then lifted her tear-wet face to his with gentle fingers. 'I've been such a fool for all these years,' he told her. 'I should never have left you after that night. It seems so long ago now, and when I think of it, we just seemed so young. But God knows we've both paid for my stupidity.'

She opened her mouth to reply, but whatever she had been going to say was stopped by the shrilling of the telephone.

Jake tore the receiver off the hook. 'Yes?' he snapped and then, his face deadpan, held it out to her. 'One of your old flames, I believe,' he said coldly. 'Gerry.'

She took the phone with trembling fingers. 'No, it isn't a good time,' she said into the mouthpiece, her eyes flickering nervously to Jake's set face. 'Tomorrow? Oh, yes, OK. One o'clock at Lorenzo's. See you then.' She put the phone down and turned to Jake. 'That was Gerry,' she said unnecessarily.

'So I gathered,' he replied drily. 'Is that the latest in your line of conquests?'

She stared at him uncomprehendingly. 'Gerry doesn't mean anything to me,' she said.

'Like all the other men you go out with, I suppose,' he grated.

Her mouth dropped open. Why was he suddenly being so prickly and unreasonable? 'Thats unfair,' she whispered.

'Is it?' he said tersely.

She stood abruptly. 'Who I see and what I think of them have nothing to do with you,' she replied defiantly.

He rose too, and looked at her for a long moment. 'I still can't figure you out, Sara,' he admitted. 'It's like opening one of those Russian dolls. You solve one mystery and there's another one underneath.'

'Nobody asked you to solve anything,' she retorted.

'True,' he said nodding. 'But you know something about those dolls?'

She shook her head and he gave her a piercing look. 'Take away the mystery and they're all empty inside.'

Sara glared back at him. 'I don't know why I let you in here,' she said, her voice wobbling in an effort to keep calm. 'You can always talk anybody into anything,' she accused. 'And then when you've got what you wanted, you just go back to being the most arrogant, insulting man in the universe. I told myself over and over what you were really like, but I didn't listen. And look where it's got me.'

'Maybe you should try picking someone more reasonable to give you advice,' he said smoothly.

'Reasonable?' she spluttered furiously. 'You mean you, for example, I suppose. You're being about as reasonable at the moment as an income tax inspector with an ulcer.'

Jake glanced at his watch. 'I'd love to stand here and listen to some more of your insults,' he said, 'but I've got work piling up.'

'Don't let me keep you,' snapped Sara.

He put two fingers under her chin and lifted her face to his. 'Get some sleep, Sara. I shall come round to-morrow and take you out to lunch. We have unfinished business to discuss.'

'I'm afraid I already have a lunch date for tomorrow,' she said coldly. 'With Gerry.'

'Cancel it,' he barked. 'This is important.'

'You are unbelievable,' she gasped.

'That makes two of us, then,' he drawled. 'I'll pick you up at one. And you better be ready.'

She stared at him wordlessly, her heart thumping at his closeness, her mind seething at his attitude.

'How long have you been seeing him?' Jake asked.

'Who?' she said unthinkingly.

He smiled. 'Gerry, your unbreakable lunch date.'

'It's none of your business,' she retorted, trying to shake off his spell.

'Everything about you is my business,' he replied. 'Especially when you keep being seen in the company of some very dodgy men. Most of whom I wouldn't trust with a bent penny.'

The absolute cheek of the man! 'I think you should go now,' she grated. 'After all, it wouldn't do to keep Emma waiting.'

He stared at her for a long moment and then grinned dazzlingly. 'Unfortunately, Emma is otherwise engaged at the moment,' he said softly.

'What a shame for you,' Sara taunted. Why did he have to be so devastatingly attractive? It just wasn't fair. But then Jake was never fair.

'You better be on time tomorrow,' he said silkily. 'It seems like we have a lot to discuss.'

When she looked him straight in the eyes, her ready retort died on her lips. There was something in his gaze that didn't fit with the flippancy of his words. Impulsively she put a hand on his arm. 'Jake. About Gerry—'

'Spare me the details,' he drawled, walking to the door. 'Get some sleep. I'll see you tomorrow at one.'

'Not if I see you first,' muttered Sara as he pulled open the door and let himself out of the flat.

Left alone once more, she stalked up and down her sitting room like a caged cheetah until her anger cooled. Why did she always have to let him wind her up like this? He was treating her as if she were some sort of possession, when they both knew that he and Emma were having an affair.

Emma. She glanced at her watch and swore softly. She should have rung in ages ago to make sure they were happy with her piece. Hurriedly she picked up the phone and dialled the office.

'Your piece was fine,' said one of her colleagues. 'But Emma's not here at the moment. She's gone out to order her wedding dress.'

Sara's whole body stilled. 'Wedding dress?' she repeated.

'Yes,' said the girl. 'And what an engagement ring. It's really beautiful. Apparently they bought it in Nepal. It's so—' But Sara had put down the phone and was staring numbly at the carpet.

Jake and Emma. Just saying their names in one breath was torture. How could he marry her? How could he? Couldn't he see she was only after him because of his money and status?

Nobody could love Jake like she did, Sara thought fiercely, throwing herself onto her bed. But it was no good. He'd obviously made up his mind.

Her mind ranged over their conversation. How dare he ask her to lunch? she thought furiously. And not just ask, but order her. She clenched her jaw. She was damned if she was going anywhere with Jake Armstrong.

Putting her head under a pillow and feeling more miserable than she would ever have thought possible, her mind finally gave way to her overwhelming tiredness and she fell asleep.

CHAPTER TEN

SARA stared at her watch and tried to control the panicky thumping of her pulse. Jake had said he would pick her up at one. But she was not going to be waiting for him.

How many people had ever stood up Jake? she wondered, and bit back the impulse to laugh hysterically at the idea of how he would react. Unfavourably would probably be the understatement of the century.

She was simply not going to be ordered about by him, especially considering he was getting married to Emma. Talk about arrogance. Jake had it in barrow-loads.

She stared at her word processor and once more unseeingly round her flat. The book she had expended so much time and effort on suddenly seemed awfully dull.

It was called *The Insider's Guide To Showbiz*, and she had spent weeks interviewing famous and not-so-famous celebrities. A few, like the 'loud-mouthed poseur' that Jake had seen lunching with her had proved simply to be a waste of time.

Others, like Gerry, the man she was meeting with today, might prove more worthwhile. He seemed pretty shady, but several people had recommended him to her because of his contacts. She sighed and glanced once more at her watch. It was ages before Jake was due to pick her up. Switching off the machine, she looked at her reflection in the mirror above the fireplace.

Once again she looked immaculate, but the eyes that gazed back at her from the reflection had a depth of expression that had not been there a week ago.

Damn Jake Armstrong, she thought with explos-
iveness. And grabbing her handbag, she slammed out
of her flat as if the hounds of hell were after her.

Gerry seemed perfectly pleasant to begin with, but as
they studied their menus in the busy little Italian restaurant she had chosen, she began to wish she had never
met him.

It was the way he kept moving his chair closer and
closer as they studied their menus and then touching her
arm when he wanted to illustrate a point that, especially
in her present agitated state, made her want to leap up
and scream.

The next time he does it, she found herself thinking,
I'll drop my drink in his lap.

Then, with a bolt of pure horror, she raised her eyes
from the menu straight into Jake's.

'What the hell do you think you're doing here?' he
demanded, pulling out a chair, but not sitting down. 'We
had a date, remember?'

Sara licked dry lips. 'You've got no right—' she began.

'Tell me,' Jake drawled, turning his shotgun stare on
Gerry, 'is that tie of yours supposed to look like that,
or is that pattern the remains of an egg you had for
breakfast last week?'

Gerry stood up. 'Who the hell are you?' he said, not
quite able to keep his voice steady as Jake stared him
down.

Jake looked at him stonily. 'I am a man whose patience
has just run out,' he bit out. 'And you are having lunch
with the woman I love.'

The words seared across Sara's brain. Love? She gazed
up at Jake and thought that the world had just stopped.
She was so shocked she couldn't think of a single
word to say.

Gerry looked from one to the other of them. 'But we were having lunch,' he said confusedly. 'I—'

' "Were" being the operative word,' Jake cut in. 'I'd be extremely grateful if you went away. I want to propose.'

Gerry stood irresolutely and then, glancing once more at Jake, began gathering up his Filofax and his mobile phone.

'You can't go!' Sara burst out, unable to stand any more.

'You heard the man,' Gerry said reasonably. 'He wants to propose to you. Who am I to stand in the way of true love?'

'But it's ridiculous!' she yelled, and then realizing the whole restaurant was looking at them, glared at Jake. 'You're just being obnoxious,' she accused. 'I suppose it's your twisted idea of revenge, just because I stood you up for lunch. You know you don't mean any of it.'

Gerry shrugged on his jacket. 'He looks pretty serious to me,' he remarked to no one in particular.

'Oh, shut up,' Sara snapped, suddenly close to tears. 'He's actually getting married to someone else.'

Jake's eyebrows rose. 'Who?' he demanded.

Sara thumped her menu. 'What do you mean, who?' she demanded in turn. 'Everyone knows you're getting married to Emma.' She looked at Gerry and added conversationally, 'The engagement ring's beautiful, you know. They bought it in Nepal.'

'I am not getting married to Emma,' grated Jake.

'Yes, you are,' contradicted Sara. 'Don't try to deny it. The entire office is awash with the latest details of her wedding dress.'

Gerry gazed narrowly from one to the other. 'Do you really know this man, Sara?' he inquired.

'Know her?' Jake echoed silkily. 'I should say so. We've been locked up in a hotel bedroom for the past week.'

'That's a damn lie,' spat Sara. 'It was only a couple of days and we weren't locked up.' She shrugged angrily. 'Not unless you count the bit before the bomb went off.'

'Bomb,' Gerry repeated faintly.

Sara stared at Jake. 'If you don't go away now,' she grated, 'I'll empty the contents of the dessert trolley on your head.'

'Such violence,' mused Jake.

'I think you're both mad,' said Gerry.

Sara glanced at him. 'Don't you dare go,' she snapped, suddenly unaccountably scared at the idea of being on her own with Jake.

Gerry shook his head. 'I can't deal with this,' he replied. 'But I think you'll both be very happy together.' And taking one final look at the two of them, he fled.

'Thank God for that,' sighed Jake, sitting in Gerry's chair. 'Shall I order? I had to get up at the crack of dawn this morning for a wedding rehearsal and I'm starving.'

Sara glared at him. 'So there is going to be a wedding, isn't there?' Tears were spurting into her eyes, but before he could reply, she added angrily, 'You come into my life and do all these things just to wind me up, don't you?' She blinked furiously. 'Why, Jake?'

The look on his face was deadly serious now. 'Sara,' he began, 'listen to me.'

'I'm not going to listen to you,' she ground out. 'I've got work to do.'

'I thought you rang in to say you were going to be off sick for the foreseeable future,' he observed mildly.

Sara's jaw dropped. She had forgotten Jake was now her boss. 'It's not that kind of work,' she mumbled.

'What kind of work, then?' he probed. 'Housework?' He shook his head. 'Unlikely. You're too disorganized.' He ignored Sara's splutterings and continued, 'Homework?' He raised an eyebrow inquiringly. 'Don't tell me. You're doing an Open University degree in syntax and basic spelling?'

'If you must know,' she ground out, tried beyond patience, 'I'm writing a book. And that man you've just seen off was one of my interviewees. He has brilliant contacts.'

He looked at her seriously. 'What kind of book?'

'It's about showbiz,' she said reluctantly. 'I've called it an insider's guide.' She shrugged. 'I don't expect you to like it. You've made it perfectly plain how all that sort of stuff bores the pants off you.'

She swirled the ice round in her glass. 'To tell you the truth,' she admitted, 'ever since I've got back from Bandhuł I can't drum up any interest in it, either.

'You were right when you called that idiot you saw me having lunch with a few weeks ago a loud-mouthed poseur. I thought what he had to say was really inter-esting, but I read it over today and he was so clichéd I glazed over halfway through.'

'So all these awful men you've been seen with recently have been contacts for your book?' Jake inquired softly, his thumb and forefinger smoothing up and down the stem of his wineglass.

'Mostly,' replied Sara. 'Although I do get asked out occasionally, you know. I'm not entirely unattractive.' Their eyes met and her face began to flood with colour. 'Not that it's any of your business,' she burst out. 'Seeing as you're getting married to my unspeakable boss.'

She was so attracted to him it was unbearable. How could he keep barging in on her life like this?

Standing up abruptly, she knocked over her glass. For one horrified moment, she stared at the widening red stain as the wine spread like a pool of blood on the crisp white tablecloth, and with a muffled gasp, she turned tail and ran out of the restaurant.

She didn't know how long she spent wandering around Kensington Gardens, one thought following another in a never-ending circle of sickening inevitability. She loved Jake, but he loved someone else. Someone she didn't even like very much.

And the way he kept popping up in her life was so unfair. Like showing a thirsty woman a glass of water she couldn't have. Only she needed Jake much worse than a drink of water. He was beginning to be as necessary to her as air.

If only she was being sent to Bandhul with him now. How different everything could be. She had had the opportunity handed to her on a plate, and she had been too blind and too proud to do anything about it.

Shivering slightly as evening drew on, she left the park and hailed a taxi. '*The Globe*, please,' she ordered.

'Brilliant,' enthused Emma, ushering her into her office.

Sara looked at her in amazement. 'Come again?' she said, sitting down as though she'd been stunned.

'Your colour piece on the Bandhul rebellion,' raved Emma. 'Absolutely brilliant.' She sat down and stretched her fingers out so she could admire the perfect lustre of her nail varnish. 'The editor loved it all, you know.'

'The editor?' echoed Sara, still not able to take in her boss's words. The Bandhul trip seemed as if it had happened three million years ago.

'You know, Sam, our editor,' replied Emma, a tinge of exasperation creeping into her voice. 'The man nominally in charge of this newspaper's editorial output. Of course,' she added shrugging, 'it could be partly because Jake took the pictures and he does happen to own the paper. But maybe I'm being too cynical.'

Sara stared at her, trying hard not to imagine her marrying Jake. 'You can never be too cynical in this office,' she said at last.

'Quite,' observed Emma, looking at her oddly. 'However, it's not just the editor. We've had a lot of calls from people saying how good they thought it was. Of course, Jake's pictures were marvellous and we absolutely flattened the opposition. Everybody else was caught completely on the hop.'

Sara sighed wearily. 'It doesn't alter the situation in the country, though, does it?' she said. 'Jake and I were lucky—we got out. But every time I close my eyes I think of how awful it was there.'

'Haven't you heard?' demanded Emma.

'What?' Sara said dully.

'The dictatorship has been overthrown. The UN has begun organizing elections for next year.'

Some of the tension in Sara's body relaxed. Perhaps her job hadn't been in vain after all. 'That's fantastic,' she said, 'but I'm still resigning.'

'Great, great,' encouraged Emma, who was not listening. 'Now, about your next job—'

'I said, I'm resigning,' Sara tried again in a slightly louder voice. 'As of now. I'm taking all my holidays in lieu of notice.'

This time Emma heard. 'What?' she demanded. 'Don't be silly. You can't. You're the flavour of the month.'

'I don't care if I'm monosodium glutamate,' Sara replied tiredly. 'I've had enough and I'm off.'

Emma smiled at her. It was not something she normally tried on Sara, but it was her grade A smile, designed to melt the frostiest situation. 'Why don't you just take tomorrow off? You'll feel better in the morning.'

Sara stared at her defiantly. 'You and this newspaper and Mr Jake Armstrong, comfortably installed in his penthouse office upstairs, have had all you are going to get out of me, Emma.'

There was a little pause. 'Well, I'm sorry to hear that,' Emma remarked with surprising sincerity. 'I was going to recommend you for my job.'

Sara's jaw dropped. 'You're giving up work? But you're so amb... I mean, you're so keen. You seem to like this job so much.'

'True,' Emma said with a little sigh. 'But things change. And I can hardly stay here working all hours while Jean Paul is racing everywhere from Brazil to Brands Hatch.'

'Well, that's very noble of you, but—' Sara stopped abruptly. 'Who did you say just then?' she asked.

'Jean Paul,' replied Emma. 'My fiancé.'

'But you're marrying Jake,' Sara burst out.

Emma smiled at her. 'I know who I'm marrying, Sara.' She leaned forward and said conspiratorially, 'Mind you, if Jean doesn't turn up, which he most certainly will, I suppose tradition would demand that Jake might have to step in, seeing as he's best man.'

Sara sat back in her chair, unable to stop staring at Emma—or even to begin understanding all the implications of what her boss had just said.

'Jean Paul, the racing driver?' she inquired rather unsteadily.

'That's right,' Emma acknowledged. 'I met him for lunch that day you had to go to Bandhul.' She blushed and Sara could only gaze at her in growing amazement.

Emma was obviously in love in a big way. 'It was love at first sight,' her boss admitted.

'But what about Jake?' objected Sara. 'Your "relationship" that you were so keen to tell me about?' She shook her head. It was all too confusing. 'You were awfully uptight about it when you were telling me I had to go to Bandhul with him,' she added.

'Oh, that was all over ages before I would admit it,' said Emma. 'Jake is very attractive, and I was jealous when he wanted to take you to Bandhul. I knew I didn't love him. I just couldn't bear the fact that he loved you.'

'Me?' Sara burst out.

Emma looked surprised. 'Of course you. Who else? I thought it was obvious. Everyone knew. It was only a question of how long. I even heard the sports department had opened a book on it.' She smiled wryly. 'Although you better not tell Jake that.'

'But he was so rotten to me,' objected Sara.

Emma grinned. 'Unmistakable sign of true love,' she said. 'Jean Paul was rude to me right through the starter and main course at that lunch. I nearly up-ended the cream jug over his head because he was so infuriating. But somehow I didn't want to walk away, and when we got to the coffee he asked me out and I just couldn't resist.' She sighed and smiled again. 'I suppose you think it's all very silly, seeing me like this.'

'No, no,' contradicted Sara. 'It's only that you came to Kathmandu,' she rejoined. 'And you called Jake "darling".'

Emma leaned across and squeezed her arm. 'Darling, I call everyone darling.' She smiled affectionately at her. 'You have got it bad, haven't you?'

'Why did you come to Kathmandu?' pressed Sara.

'Because I was ordered to,' replied Emma. 'And when Jake's father is in a monumental strop and says, "jump," one's only reply is "how high?" ' She smiled. 'But it was nice. Jean Paul came with me.'

'I didn't see him,' gasped Sara.

'You were only around for five minutes before you did your disappearing act,' noted Emma. 'I came to give you your passports, and then Jean Paul and I were supposed to be going out to dinner.

'When Jake found you had gone, he went absolutely spare. I thought he was going to murder the waiter, the hotel receptionist and the woman manning the check-in desk at the airport. In that order.

'Of course, Jean Paul has such a Latin temperament he joined in, as well, and after Jake had made certain you were safely on the plane, they ended up going on a monumental bender and swopping stories of the fickleness of women in general and you and me in particular.'

She smiled again. 'Didn't stop him catching the next available plane, though. Boy, was he furious with you.'

Sara gazed at her happy face and realized enviously that Emma hadn't actually stopped smiling since they'd met in the corridor ten minutes before. Why did everyone around her have to look so full of joy when she felt so confused and miserable?

'I'm surprised Jake didn't tell you he was going to be best man,' Emma continued. 'He said he was going to see you, so I gave him your invitation.'

Sara swallowed. 'We didn't get round to discussing it,' she said lamely. 'I'm sorry I spoiled your evening in Kathmandu,' she added.

'Not at all,' Emma said warmly. 'I had a whale of a time. I suddenly realized the fun I've been missing out on all my life.' She waved a hand at her desk. 'That's why I'm resigning,' she said. 'I want to start living.'

*   *   *

Sara got into the lift and pressed the button for the top floor. She was shaking so much she was surprised the lift didn't rattle. Jake loved her, Emma had said. But he had lied to her. Made her feel angry and foolish and more jealous than anyone had a right to.

She didn't know whether to throw herself into his arms or to see that he fried in hell. Maybe he wouldn't see her, she thought in sudden panic. She clasped her hands together. She'd make him see her if it was the last thing she did.

Jake was sitting at his desk, a mountain of papers in front of him. He didn't even look up as Sara powered through the door, his secretary hurrying after her. 'Mr Armstrong is not to be disturbed,' she said, trying to grab hold of Sara's shoulder. 'He gave strict instructions—'

But Jake was on his feet coming towards her. 'Where the hell have you been?' he grated. 'Do you know how worried I've been about you?'

His secretary looked at them both and then let herself discreetly out of the office.

Sara looked at Jake's set face and felt a sudden shaft of uncertainty.

'Sara,' he said softly.

She swallowed. 'I'm glad you're wearing black,' she heard herself saying, her carefully prepared, oh so reasonably worded speech flying out the window. 'It's a particularly good colour for a funeral. Yours.'

'All that time you spent lounging about at home doesn't seem to have done much for your temper,' he drawled.

'It was all the unwanted callers I kept getting,' she grated. 'I've just seen Emma. How dare you lie to me about the wedding?'

He looked at her steadily. 'I didn't lie to you. You misled yourself. And then you ran off before I had the chance to explain.'

She glared at him. 'I only ran off because—' She stopped abruptly.

'Because what?' he prompted gently. His eyes were so soft she could fall into them any moment, she found herself thinking.

She refocused suddenly and clenched her jaw. 'I'm resigning,' she forced out. 'I just can't handle this any more. I don't know how to feel or how to act when I'm around you. Maybe it's better that I go.'

'Where?' he demanded, stepping right up to her.

'I don't know,' she said wildly, unnerved by his nearness. 'Anywhere. I don't care any more.'

Her heart was beating so loudly she was certain he could hear it. Whirling round, she fled for the door.

But he was too quick for her. 'I don't think so,' he said firmly blocking her way. 'You're not running away from me twice in one day. Do you know the terrible things that would do to my reputation?'

'Damn your reputation,' she breathed furiously. He was just too close.

'Sara,' he said softly, 'don't you want to hear that you're the most beautiful woman I've ever seen?'

'That's just the sort of stupid remark I'd expect you to come out with,' she retorted, not listening as she tried to lunge past him for the doorknob.

He grasped her by both arms and shook her slightly. 'Goddammit, woman,' he said exasperatedly, 'can't you see I love you? How many times do I have to tell you before you believe me?'

'Let me go,' she said, struggling. 'You—' She stopped and looked up into his face. 'Wh-what did you say?' she faltered.

'I love you,' he repeated tenderly, his fingers stroking through her hair. 'God knows I've treated you abominably, and I don't expect you to forgive me, but I can't help thinking you feel the same way about me.' He gazed at her for a long moment. 'Am I right?'

Her whole body stilled and she reached up to touch his face.

'I'll take that for a yes, shall I?' he murmured.

'Yes,' she choked out. 'You know I love you. I told you in Bandhul but you only laughed in my face. So what's different now?'

'I am,' he replied simply. 'I wanted to hate you, Sara. I certainly tried hard enough over the years. You kept avoiding me, and then when I thought you were in love with Jamie, I felt just like I'd been stabbed in the heart.

'I never understood why you never contacted me. I never thought that it was simply because you hadn't got my note and the ticket. I thought you were punishing me. At first I felt consumed with guilt because, after all, you were so young. But then, when I heard about Jamie's death, I got angry. So angry. I wanted to hurt you like you'd hurt me.'

He reached behind him and, locking the door, carried her over to the brown leather chesterfield in the corner of his office.

'I can't do without you, Sara. God knows I've tried. Every time I saw you in the office, I ached to carry you off somewhere like some demented caveman. Even what happened to Jamie—'

She laid gentle fingers across his lips and he grasped them.

'I behaved so horribly towards you because I hated myself for wanting you so much. Wanting somebody who I thought had treated us both so appallingly,' he said quietly. He raked his fingers through his hair. 'I was so jealous of him,' he added.

'There was no need to be,' Sara said gently.

'I know that now,' he whispered, his blue-black gaze enveloping her. His fingers trailed down her throat. 'I want you so much I can't remember when I didn't feel like this.'

'Me, too,' Sara gasped before her words were stopped with a kiss. His hands slowly undid the buttons of her suit jacket and then reached inside. 'Jake,' she sighed, the blood thundering in her ears, her hands reaching round his neck.

He looked up at her, his eyes glittering with desire. 'You don't need to say it,' he told her heatedly. 'I'll never leave you again. I've been a fool all these years, and now I'm going to make up for it.'

The morning sun filtered through the hotel curtains and Sara moved sleepily against Jake, her hands loving the silkiness of his warm skin. Her eyes blinked against the light and she sighed contentedly.

'Great wedding,' she murmured as Jake's arms slid round her. He kissed her throat and her hands framed his face. 'Sure you don't regret marrying me?' she teased playfully.

'Would you like me to prove it to you?' he demanded huskily.

'Oh, yes,' she sighed.

It was late afternoon when he turned her face to his and asked softly, 'Why so sad, Sara? What's the matter?'

She shook her head slightly. 'It's silly,' she said at last.

'Out with it,' he pressed.

'It's just that I remember how unhappy you looked in Nepal when you were talking about going to work in an office every day,' she said in a rush. 'Is that really what you want, Jake?'

'Who said anything about an office?' he drawled, his fingers sliding down her spine.

'But—but you're in charge of the company now,' she managed to return, her thoughts beginning to unravel as he pulled her closer.

'My father's feeling so much better he's going to give it another year,' he said. 'I thought I'd use it to go out in a big way, so I'm planning to do a photographic safari in Africa.'

She drew back in surprise. 'Africa?' she echoed.

He nodded expressionlessly.

'How long will you be away?' she asked shakily.

Jake shrugged. 'At least six months,' he said. 'And I've thought of a great writer to do the text. Of course,' he added seriously, 'she'd have to come with me. I hope you don't mind.'

Sara swallowed hard. 'Who?' she whispered.

'You, of course,' replied Jake. 'It'll make a perfect honeymoon.'

MILLS & BOON®

Next Month's Romances

♡

Each month you can choose from a wide variety of romance with Mills & Boon. Below are the new titles to look out for next month in our two new series Presents and Enchanted.

Presents™

THEIR WEDDING DAY	Emma Darcy
THE FINAL PROPOSAL	Robyn Donald
HIS BABY!	Sharon Kendrick
MARRIED FOR REAL	Lindsay Armstrong
MISTLETOE MAN	Kathleen O'Brien
BAD INFLUENCE	Susanne McCarthy
TORN BY DESIRE	Natalie Fox
POWERFUL PERSUASION	Margaret Mayo

Enchanted™

THE VICAR'S DAUGHTER	Betty Neels
BECAUSE OF THE BABY	Debbie Macomber
UNEXPECTED ENGAGEMENT	Jessica Steele
BORROWED WIFE	Patricia Wilson
ANGEL BRIDE	Barbara McMahon
A WIFE FOR CHRISTMAS	Pamela Bauer & Judy Kaye
ALL SHE WANTS FOR CHRISTMAS	Liz Fielding
TROUBLE IN PARADISE	Grace Green

SINGLE LETTER SWITCH

A year's supply of Mills & Boon Presents™ novels— absolutely FREE!

Would you like to win a year's supply of passionate compelling and provocative romances? Well, you can and the're free! Simply complete the grid below and send it to us by 31st May 1997. The first five correct entries picked after the closing date will win a year's supply of Mills & Boon Presents™ novels (six books every month—worth over £150). What could be easier?

S	T	O	C	K
P	L	A	T	E

Clues:

A   To pile up
B   To ease off or a reduction
C   A dark colour
D   Empty or missing
E   A piece of wood
F   Common abbreviation for an aircraft

Please turn over for details of how to enter ☞

How to enter...

There are two five letter words provided in the grid overleaf. The first one being STOCK the other PLATE. All you have to do is write down the words that are missing by changing just one letter at a time to form a new word and eventually change the word STOCK into PLATE. You only have eight chances but we have supplied you with clues as to what each one is. Good Luck!

When you have completed the grid don't forget to fill in your name and address in the space provided below and pop this page into an envelope (you don't even need a stamp) and post it today. Hurry—competition ends 31st May 1997.

Mills & Boon® Single Letter Switch
FREEPOST
Croydon
Surrey
CR9 3WZ

Are you a Reader Service Subscriber?   Yes ☐   No ☐

Ms/Mrs/Miss/Mr _____

Address _____

_____

_____ Postcode _____

One application per household.

C6K